the
One-legged
Man

...who came out of a well

TO: TONY

MOSTLY OIL AND WATER
COME FROM WELLS...
BUT NOW AND OTHEN —

All The best,

Bent H. Wood

2010

First Edition

Text set in Bodoni Book
Copyright 2001 by Robert Holland
Printed on acid-free paper in Canada
ISBN 0 - 9658523-9-3

Cover and title page design and illustrations by
Robert J. Benson

Frost Hollow Publishers,LLC
411 Barlow Cemetery Road
Woodstock, CT 06281
phone: 860-974-2081
fax: 860-974-0813
email:frstholw@neca.com
website: frosthollowpub.com

the One-legged Man

...who came out of a well

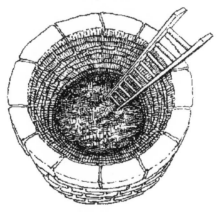

A novel of Sports and Mystery by

Robert Holland

FROST HOLLOW
PUBLISHERS, LLC

Woodstock, Connecticut

More books for
teen and middle readers
By
Robert Holland

The Voice of the Tree
The Purple Car
Summer on Kidd's Creek
Footballs Never Bounce True
Breakin' Stones
Eben Stroud
Harry the Hook
Mad Max Murphy

Check your local bookseller or order directly from Frost Hollow. Call toll free at 877-974-2081.

All the above titles are $10.95 except for Harry The Hook, which is $11.95. Shipping and handling and sales tax extra.

Also check out our web site at frosthollowpub.com. Read about the books in the series and find out what's coming next.

ONE

Me, Nick Rivers

Adults are crazy. I don't mean crazy like locked away in a bad-brain bin crazy, but just sort of like some of their wires get crossed once they have kids to deal with. The reason I know this is because we had a section on genetics in biology and the teacher made it clear that people haven't changed in a long, long, long time. So that means that when adults were kids they acted the way kids do now, which also means that their problems started when they stopped being kids and started thinking of themselves as adults.

What happens is that they start taking everything seriously. My dad is a good example. Everything is a crisis. One bad grade and he starts frowning and lecturing, and while I could live with furrowed brows and a pout, the lectures are unbearable. Does he think I don't know I screwed up? I know I screwed up. I'm supposed to screw up. I'm a kid! It's in my contract. But do I get any credit for knowing anything? Forget about it. He just goes on and on, lecturing away about how I'm not taking my future seriously, wasting time with a lecture when I could be playing video games.

What is the future anyway? Nothing more than what happens when you wake up in the morning. By afternoon it's history. It's done with. The future is what clothes you put on that day, what happens with your friends that day. Anything beyond that and you need a fortune teller.

My mother doesn't lecture at all. She doesn't have to. She just sighs and wonders aloud where they went wrong. Solid gold guilt. It's enough to make me puke. And there's nothing you can do about it except leave, and they know that's not really an alternative because you can't do that without a job and a car and someone to cook for you and take care of your laundry and stuff like that. I mean, figure it out. Video games go for around sixty-four bucks a pop and there's no way I can get a job that would keep me in rent, gas, insurance, food, clothes, shoes, and video games.

Of course, I could do everything they want and then the lectures would stop and the guilt trips would end, but then I wouldn't be me. I'd just be a walking-around-zombie who was only what other people thought I ought to be. I don't know what you think about that, but I can tell you, I am an independent human being and it is my right to live like one.

Well, that's the way my thinking has gone for a long time. The only trouble with thinking that way is that it depresses me and there is no point in being depressed. You miss too much. Like when I was on Ritalin. I missed a lot then, which was why when I was ten I stopped taking it. They thought I was taking it, but I just hid the pills and then after about a year without any complaints from my goofball teachers about being too aggressive and too loud and too talkative and not being able to sit still in class, I dumped the whole bag of pills on the table one day and told my mother that I wasn't taking any more drugs.

What could they say? They had to agree, especially after I pointed out that getting people used to the idea of using drugs to solve their problems was a bad idea and would probably lead to them to start taking other drugs, like marijuana and stuff like that. I was, of course, careful not to mention that alcohol is a drug, because adults get very grumpy when you mention that. They just can't live with the idea that a martini with three olives is a drug. *It's a martini, dammit, and there's nothing wrong with a martini (or two) after a hard day at the office.* Have you ever tasted a martini? Try a sip and tell me that isn't a drug. It has to be. Drugs taste bad. Like cough medicine. Or try this one. Scotch. That ranks right up there with liver as far as I'm concerned. Beer's okay though. I've tried beer. Everybody I know has tried beer. It's the beverage of choice, like Pepsi or Coke. It depends on what kind of a kick you want, caffeine or alcohol, take your pick. The only problem with beer is that if you drink too much, or if you drink even a little and drink it too fast, you wind up puking and then the next day you feel like you've got the flu, so my advice in this is don't drink. And, of course, only the dumbest jerk in the world drinks and then drives. You could lose your license that way.

Before I get too far into this, maybe you ought to know something about me. First off, my name is Nick Rivers and I think I'm pretty cool, but I suppose there's some disagreement about that, especially from my older sister Beth who is eighteen and in her first year of college. Couldn't have happened soon enough. It was like having two mothers; one who attacked me for not being cool and one who nagged me to pick up my room so I'd be successful in the future. I told you adults are crazy. I have a second sister, Lizzie, who is ten and is perfectly nice most of the time.

I'm sixteen. I've got my license but I don't have a car because we've already got two cars. I'm pretty sure Dad could afford to get a car for Beth and one for me, but he's "morally opposed" to spending that much money on kids. It's a point upon which I'm not sure he and Mother agree. He takes his car and goes to work and she taxis the rest of us all over town, grumbling each way about having to drive us everywhere. Both Beth and I have been saving money for years. I cut lawns and shovel snow and even use the snow thrower on the tractor to clear four driveways. But even for all of that I've only got about three thousand saved and that includes Christmas presents from both sets of grandparents, so I'm guessing here that I'll be all the way through college before I have enough money for a car.

Here's some more information about me. I'm almost five foot eleven, I've got blue eyes, light brown hair (straight), and I weigh one hundred and sixty-five pounds. I'm now the starting shortstop for my high school baseball team, and I'm a pretty good hitter, but at the start of the season I was riding the bench. I'm a good enough student and I'm getting better. I do best in math and science, but I also do well in English, as you can tell from the high quality of the writing you are reading. My teacher doesn't like it, though, too chatty, she says. Screw her. She thinks J.D. Salinger is a good writer and he only wrote the dumbest book I ever read, and I read a lot. Tolkien is my favorite. There is nothing like *The Lord of the Rings* and there never will be. I read it at least once a year and I've been doing that since I was nine.

I've got two good friends, Ronnie Lathrop, and Paul Hunter, and I'm really, really good at video games. Nobody can beat me, at least anybody I know or anybody who hangs out at the arcade at the mall. Any game. You pick it and you'll find my name at the top. As you can see, all the stuff I do, along with fishing and hunting (which I'll be starting this fall) is not the stuff girls think is cool. But let me tell you what I know about that. Girls don't think anything boys do is cool unless it means they are paying attention to girls. Probably that sounds a little cynical but I've been male my whole life and I've got sisters on either side of me and I've spent a lot of time listening, which turns out to be a pretty good way to learn about people.

And that idea leads to what this book is all about because it was by watching and listening that I first noticed Mr. Bede who lives up the road from us. We live sort of in the country in a section of town where there are still some farms and the houses are pretty well spread out. Most of the people live in subdivisions.

As it turns out, Mr. Bede's house sits on a hill and I can see it from the window in my room, and I have this monster telescope that I got two Christmases ago. Then one night, by accident, I happened to focus on Mr. Bede's house. Through the windows I saw him making something ... something big, but all I could tell was that it was big and made from metal of some kind. I must've watched for an hour and all he did was put things together and then take them apart and put them together again.

What struck me was that he was doing this in what should have been his living room, and we all know what a living room is. That's where nobody lives. It is kept like a museum or maybe a furniture store window. You can't sit on the furniture in your regular clothes, you can't take a soda in there. Weird. Totally weird. Not that anyone wants to go into a living room anyway because there's nothing to do in there. No TV, no books, nothing. Only adults go into living rooms. Enough said.

But there was Mr. Bede working in his living room like it was some sort of metal shop. I could see some big machines there, but I didn't know what they were.

Before that I had never thought much about Mr. Bede. He was just a neighbor who had a lot of junk in his yard that my mother complained about all the time because it looked pretty messy, even by my standards,which according to my mother borders on basic dump. But hey, does it make any sense to put stuff in drawers? All you do is take it back out. I'll bet in a lifetime, you'd waste a couple of months just opening and closing drawers and closets. I pile my socks in one place, underwear in another, jeans and tees in another. I know where everything is and I can tell at a glance when my supply is getting low and that's when I lug the dirty stuff down to the laundry.

But anyway, the next night at dinner, I asked about Mr. Bede.

"That awful old man!" my mother said. "He's a disgrace!

Somebody ought to make him clean up his yard, at least."

"But nobody will," Dad said.

"Of course not. They're all scared of him, with all his fancy degrees and the fact that his family has lived here for three hundred years. Maybe I ought to start a campaign."

I assumed from the tone of the conversation that he must have broken all ten commandments and then thrown in a couple of extra just to make sure he'd got it done right, because there's nothing like breaking rules to drive adults wild, even if the only rules you break are the same ones they break.

"Wow," I said, "pretty strange guy, huh?"

"Eccentric," Dad said.

"What do you know about him? What's he like?"

Silence.

"Do you know him?"

"What brought this up?" Mom asked in the tone of voice that made you understand that she suspected you had some hidden plan that could get you tossed into jail for the rest of your life.

"He's a neighbor and I just wondered about him, that's all." (There's a lesson here. I could've gotten mad and shot off my mouth and given them the "you never trust me" drill, but whenever Beth did that they only got more suspicious.) "I mean, you gotta admit he's different."

"He's different all right," Dad said.

"Well, what's he like?"

"We've never spoken to him," Mom said.

"I thought you knew everybody in the neighborhood."

"Except Mr. Bede," she said.

"Hank Johnson told me," Dad said, "that he's got a degree in mechanical engineering and a law degree, and a Ph.D. in physics, so I guess he's pretty smart. He's an inventor and Hank says he holds a slew of patents. The rumor is that he has a lot of money. He used to be married and he's got a couple of kids who are grown."

"That's all?"

"What else do you need to know?" Mom asked.

I shrugged. Shrugging is excellent. Here's why. It's ambiguous. Now there's a hot vocabulary word ... real SAT type stuff.

"He's not very friendly," Mom said. "When we first moved in here and I'd see him outside I used to wave, but he never waved back. Can you imagine! Why wouldn't he wave back?"

"Probably because he didn't know you," I said.

"That's no reason not to be friendly," Mom said.

My parents came from the Midwest where people spend half their lives waving and bobbing their heads and chatting. Here in New England, where I grew up, people don't go in for that sort of stuff. As long as nobody bothers you, you don't bother them. This attitude does not sit well with Mom, and for a long time I thought she was right because I saw no reason why you shouldn't be friendly with people. As I got older I discovered that it wasn't so much friendliness she was after as nosing into other people's business.

I didn't figure that out until I was about thirteen and we went out to visit my grandparents in Ohio and all they did was sit around gossiping about everyone. I hate gossip. It's not that I don't like hearing news about what's gone on, but I just want the headlines and not all the sneaky little remarks that some people think is conversation.

"Mr. Bede must be pretty smart," I said.

"Hank says his degree in engineering is from MIT and his law degree is from Harvard and his Physics degree is also from M.I.T."

"Whoa. Sounds like a genius to me."

"Just what is this all about?" Dad asked.

"Nothing," I said, because truly, at that point, it was merely curiosity. Of course, they didn't believe me.

"Well, just stay away from there," Mom said. "Anybody who can't at least wave is someone to stay away from."

You see? Absolutely nuts. People who wave all the time aren't in the least interesting. Nothing but bobbing heads in the back windows of cars. But a man who built machines in his living room, now, that was somebody I wanted to know more about.

I tried Ronnie's parents, figuring that because they had grown up in town, they might not be so hung up on waving. They weren't, but that didn't shut off the gossip spout. That took me by surprise because I'd thought only Midwestern people gossiped. Wrong. But then I'm wrong about a lot of stuff.

"There are some very strange stories about Augustus Bede," his mother said. Plenty of people in town think he murdered his wife, but the police never did anything."

"Maybe he didn't," I said.

"Oh, that's not what a lot of people thought."

"Why would he have killed her?"

"That's just the trouble. No one ever knew."

"What about their kids?"

"Two boys. Every bit as strange and smart as their father. I don't know where they are now."

Mr. Lathrop looked up. "They both went to M.I.T. One works at Boeing and the other one works for Microsoft."

"How do you know that?" Mrs. Lathrop asked, sounding as if there were some reason not to know that.

"Tom Gray told me."

"Why would he tell you that?"

Mr. Lathrop shrugged. He might be an adult, but at least he hadn't forgotten the essential principle of being a kid. When you don't want to answer, shrug.

"Is he mean?" I asked.

The question seemed to take them by surprise.

"He lives alone," Mrs. Lathrop said.

Ronnie laughed. "What difference does that make?"

"All the difference in the world," his mother said.

"Absolutely," Mr. Lathrop said.

Almost as good as a shrug, I thought.

After that, whenever I turned my telescope on Mr. Bede's house I thought about the stories and I wondered if the man I was watching was a murderer. Over and over I told myself that he couldn't be, if only because murderers went to prison or were executed, or at the least they stood trial. But none of that had happened to Mr. Bede.

TWO

What Killed The Cat

Baseball starts in the spring and my life revolves around baseball. Since I was ten my dream has been to play second base for the Red Sox. If I lived in a different part of the country, it would probably be some other team, but here, in New England, the Red Sox rule.

Actually, by the end of most seasons, it's the Yankees who rule, but there's always hope that someday the Sox may finally escape the jinx that's plagued them ever since they sold Babe Ruth to the Yankees. There's always hope. Yeah, right ... like my actually playing for the Sox. But the way I look at it, I'm sixteen and only a sophomore so I've got plenty of time to develop my game. And if I don't get drafted out of high school, maybe I'll get drafted out of college ... maybe.

But unless my hitting improved there wouldn't even be a maybe. And unless my grades improved I wouldn't get into what my parents call a "good college". These are the kinds of things that keep kids under a lot of pressure, even though adults talk about their teenage years as if they were a history written by some dumb dude who writes girlie movies where everything comes out right in the end.

Is that weird? I mean, if you've been a kid, then you must remember what it was like to be a kid, right? Like, take this past year, for example. The nastiest age ever is fifteen because all you can think about is getting your driver's license, and all you can do is ... wait. Total pressure. Does any adult remember how long a day is? I don't think so. They even think a year is a short time. NUTS! Out of touch. Try this. Every kid I know likes to stay up late and sleep in the next day. But school, which is run by adults, starts at seven-stinking-thirty in the morning. Most of the kids wake up around lunch time. But there's no point in even talking to the adults about that, so mostly I don't, because the best way to stay out of trouble is to keep your mouth shut. Let me give you an example.

I say to Mom, "Hey, Mom? I'm going over to Ronnie's."

"What for?"

Clearly a dumb question, but you have to answer, so the only thing I can do is lie because if I tell her we're going to play Nintendo, I'll get a long boring lecture on how video games "rot the mind." Where do they get that stuff? Is there some secret book where they list stuff parents are supposed to say to their kids?

"We're doing our geometry homework," I answer.

"Okay, but be back in time for supper."

We didn't do any geometry. We played video games. You don't hang out with a best buddy to do geometry, for God's sake. So I went over to Ronnie's, which is only a couple of miles down the road, and I took my bike because it beats walking, even though it is not cool to be riding a bike when you have your driver's license.

"Why did you ask my parents about Mr. Bede?" Ronnie asked as we sat on the couch in front of the TV.

"Curious, that's all."

"After you left I heard my parents talking about him. I don't think they like him very much. My mother said she thinks he's some kind of a pervert."

"Really?"

"What do you think?"

"Nothing. I just wondered about him, you know, 'cause he's an inventor and he lives by himself."

"What does he invent?"

"I don't know. What does any inventor invent? Bell invented the telephone, Edison invented the phonograph. Whitney invented the cotton gin, but I only know about those guys because they're famous. But if you think about it, I mean, there must be a lot of inventors out there and I have no idea who they are or what they invent."

Ronnie is a pretty regular guy and conversations like that are never conversations because he clams up and won't talk. We went for a round of Didi Kong Racing.

Of course, talking about Mr. Bede only made me more curious, and when I get curious I'm like a dog on a scent. I just have to know more. But the two times I'd asked adults about Mr. Bede, not only didn't I get any information, but they sent off warning signals in the same tone of voice they use when they say things like "never talk to strangers."

Good advice, but as you get older, you discover that while it makes you cautious about adults (which you should be) it also gets in the way. When you start asking questions you run out of people you know pretty fast.

The only possibility was the library. I figured Mr. Bede must have been in the newspapers at some time and libraries have collections of old newspapers. Except ours. The librarian told me I'd have to go over to UConn for that.

Which left me trying to figure out when I could borrow one of the cars and what I'd tell my parents about where I was going and why I was going there. They would immediately be suspicious if I said I was going to the library, so I needed some other excuse. And while I was working that out, I was free to concentrate on baseball.

I'm a terrific fielder, if I say so myself, and I was pretty sure I had a shot at making the varsity this year because the second baseman had graduated. I knew a couple of guys had transferred in, but neither of them played second.

There's a reason I'm a good fielder. I'm not afraid of the ball when it comes skipping across the ground. And the reason I don't back off is because two years ago I got Dad to buy me one of those bounce-backs. Then, while Dad was at work and Mom was helping with a food drive for earthquake victims in Colombia, I skinned off a piece of the back lawn, raked out all the rocks, and set up the bounce-back so when I fired a baseball at it the ball came back skipping first on the grass and then on the dirt, just the way it comes at a second baseman.

I expected I would be grounded for screwing up the lawn, but the pool, (yes, we have a pool ... it came with the house, a nice thirty-five foot pool that I love when I swim in it and hate when I have to clean it), the pool is off to the side of the house and the bedrooms and bathrooms look out the back, and it was early July and hotter than a sauna, and everybody used the pool and nobody went out back.

That lasted two weeks. In fairness, summer vacations are hard on mothers. Very hard. Lizzie hates the heat and she spends all her time sitting in the den watching TV or talking to her friends on the phone. Her best friend Marta lives just down the road, maybe a quarter of a mile or so, but neither of them will get on their bikes. They sit and talk on the phone and complain about how bored they are. Beth was making a fortune baby-sitting. I cut the grass. Nobody went into the backyard, except me, and I spent four to five hours a day out there, winging a ball at the bounce-back.

Every time I'd come in soaked with sweat, shower off, and drop into the pool, and Mom never asked what I was doing to get so sweaty. Nobody ever asked me anything as long as I stayed out from under foot. During summer vacation the only thing a mother wants is that her kids stay busy and don't plague her with wanting to go places.

Lizzie loves malls and she almost always gets to go, because Mom loves malls too. I hate malls. All they have are stores full of clothes and shiny objects. Of course that does attract girls, who I think have all the same instincts as the Indians who traded Manhattan for some shiny beads. If you need any proof of that, just go to a craft show (another torture chamber for kids) and watch the females all panting over the earrings and jewelry while the husbands stand around with their hands in their pockets.

That's why whenever I get the car I have six crystals on a string that I hang over the rearview mirror. Hey, I might be sixteen, but I'm not stupid. They want shiny objects, give 'em shiny objects. The other thing you do is let 'em talk. All you have to do is every now and then say things like, "whoa, awesome" or "that is *so* cool," or "that is so *not* cool." The less you say, the more mysterious it makes you, which is why dumb jocks are so popular.

So nobody asked what I was doing to work up such a sweat and somehow, I forgot to mention it. Then the heat wave ended and one Saturday morning I was in the middle of my workout when Dad suddenly appeared.

"What happened to the lawn?" he asked in a particularly wounded tone of voice.

For a guy with a very good job, a guy who makes a lot of money, it was a pretty dumb question. But, on the other hand, he is very big on grass. No weeds allowed. We spread chemicals, we have a built in watering system, I cut the grass and have to bag all the clippings. But as much as I hated all the work, when I went to set up my practice pit, I didn't have to do anything to the grass beyond cutting it a little shorter in front of the bounce-back.

"I needed an infield to practice on," I said.

"But, you took up a whole patch of lawn."

I kept on firing the ball and fielding it as we talked. "I needed an infield," I said.

"But couldn't you have taken your bike to the field?"

"No bounce-back."

"Couldn't Ronnie or Paul hit baseballs to you?"

"Not fast enough ...." I dove flat out for a hard liner to my right, speared it on one hop and rolled to my feet. It was a heck of a catch and I couldn't see how that wouldn't impress him, but he was focused on the missing grass.

"Don't you think you should have asked first?"

"You were at work." Another hard shot, this one to my right and I ran two steps and scooped it cleanly.

"But, Nick, I mean, when you're gonna tear up the lawn you ought to make sure it's all right."

"Okay," I said. "If I do it again, I'll be sure to ask."

He nodded, but he looked confused and you never leave an adult confused. I stopped. "Dad, next spring I want to make the team and the only way I can do that is to be the best I can be." It's a lousy line, I mean really dumb, but whoever wrote it was a genius. No parent will interfere with a kid who wants to be the best he can be. But you want to be careful not to overwork it. Save it for studies and sports.

"Well, I suppose ..."

"I can always replant the grass," I said. "If I get good enough, I can do it this fall."

"How long has this been here?"

I'd been waiting for him to ask. "A little over two weeks."

"It couldn't have been."

I had him. How could he possibly admit that he'd been too busy to notice? And what could he say to Mom?

"Does this really work?"

"Sure. Did you see those catches I made? Two weeks ago I couldn't even come close to those balls. Every day I keep increasing my range."

"How often do you work out?"

"Two hours each morning and afternoon."

"Right through that heat?"

"Every day. You wanna get good, practice." Now I really had him. He said that about everything. Not that he wasn't right, because, in fact, he was. Dead right. But nothing makes a parent feel better about their kids than to hear their own words coming back at them. You can do the same thing with teachers, but you have to listen closely to find out which words mean the most to them and then you get those words into every test and quiz and paper.

He grinned. "Well, don't let me stop you," he said. "You going for a swim in the pool after you finish?"

"You bet!"

"Well, I'll see you there."

Don't forget to shower, I said to myself.

"And don't forget to shower," he said.

"I won't, Dad."

So when tryouts came up this spring, I was ready. I could even turn the double play, no sweat. There might be a guy who could hit better and play second, but after the first day of practice the job was mine and I knew it. Coaches love defense. They talk about defense all the time, so a guy who can take hits away from the opposing team gets high marks.

Still, the hitting was a problem and what I needed was a pitching machine and a cage. Every Saturday and Sunday I went down to the batting cage in Pattendale, but it took all my allowance to pay for the gas and hit about a hundred balls.

I asked the coach what a cage cost and it was a stunner. A good machine and the cage and frame for the cage would run about three grand, as in $3,000. It would wipe out my savings. The short of it was, I put the idea far back in my mind in the place I save for dreams that Dad won't go for because he's "morally opposed" to spending "that kind of money" on kids.

After dinner, I spent the whole night studying Spanish for a big test the next day. I hate Spanish. Nobody in my family was Spanish. They all came from northern Europe. A lot of them were Germans and there were some Swedes and Norwegians and Danes too, but mostly German. Why didn't the school offer German? Here's the answer I got from the head of the language department, Miss Google. (I'll tell you one thing. If my name were Google I would get married as fast as I could. And for sure I would never never be a teacher. Kids latch right on to stuff like that. How can you take somebody named Miss Google seriously?) I knew it was useless, but I asked anyway. Here's what Miss Google told me. Everybody wants to take Spanish or French and the school couldn't afford to have a teacher who only taught German because not enough kids would take the course.

"Do you know how many kids are interested?" I asked.

"Well, no," she said, "but it isn't very high."

As you can see it wasn't only her name that was all googly.

Truth be known, I was probably better off taking Spanish. It's pretty easy and I need three years of a language for college, so I went over all the tests and quizzes.

Later, I went upstairs and plopped down behind my telescope. Mr. Bede was hard at work, walking back and forth, though, as usual, I had no idea what he was working on. I'm not even sure why I kept watching, except that there was something about the way he moved that left me thinking I was watching someone I knew. He was slow in the way he walked from place to place, but when he sat down at the bench, his hands moved quickly.

I must have been watching for a half hour or more when suddenly I began to make sense out of the strange collection of parts he had put together. It was a clock, or what looked like a clock. I mean, he was, after all, an inventor, and with guys like that you can't always count on what you see. For all I knew, he could be making a timing mechanism designed to set off a bomb .... A bomb? I pulled my eye from the scope and looked at the wall. Why not? Didn't that guy in Montana who sent bombs through the mail, didn't he also live alone. And you can bet *he* never waved back at anybody.

I put my eye back to the scope, but now the room was dark and the only light shone dimly through curtains on a window in the floor above the living room. I readjusted the scope so it looked upward toward the stars, just in case any-one got nosey, though I didn't think they would. Heck, it had taken them two weeks to find a big patch of lawn was miss-ing.

I brushed my teeth and went to bed and then lying there in the dark, looking up at my ceiling and the constellations I had arranged there with glow-in-the-dark stars, I wondered if Mr. Bede might really be making a bomb. Certainly he would know how to make one. But why would he make one?

I went over a list of reasons in my mind. Somebody he didn't like? Settling an old score? The Internal Revenue Ser-vice? Cops? Technology? Cutting off old growth forests? Abortion? It got complicated pretty fast. Any one of those reasons would be enough. It depended on what kind of a mind you were dealing with. So far all I knew was that he lived alone and invented stuff, but even with so little to go on, I was sure I was onto something. It was like suddenly smelling dog turd and then checking your shoes to see if you'd stepped in it, and even though your shoes are clean you keep smelling it. I looked ahead to Saturday. Okay, here was the excuse. I'm working on a history paper and my teacher wants me to go over to UConn to look up stuff. Sounded good. But what sort of questions would that produce? "What was the paper on?" Yeah, they'd ask that one. "How long was the paper? When was it due?" Yup, those too. They had to ask questions like that to show interest in what I was doing, though in reality they were only checking out my story. No problemo. Dunk shot. I grinned. But this time I'd remember to write down what I said so I didn't forget if the subject came up again. Always cover your trail. It's the only way.

And so, with Mom convinced that I was researching a paper for history, I went to the library.

It was a lot bigger than I had thought, and in fact, it was hard to imagine that anyone would build a building that big just to hold books.

But I'll give 'em this, they've got the place pretty well organized. I only had to ask once to find the right desk and a very nice, very helpful woman there told me just how to go about finding what I wanted. It was all stored on films that you put into a machine with a big screen. Pretty easy.

The question was what films I needed to look at. I started with the index, looking under inventors and Mr. Bede's name popped right up. I got the film, put it into the machine, and scrolled to the right page. Nothing to it. Duck soup. And then my jaw dropped as I read the headline.

Charges Dropped
Against Inventor

HARTFORD — Murder charges were dropped today against Augustus Bede, IV, and police began searching anew for the killer of Mr. Bede's wife, Mary (Parker) Bede who was killed two weeks ago.

Mrs. Bede was found by her husband when he returned from taking his two young sons, ages 8 and 6, to the doctor.

Mrs. Bede had been beaten to death with a heavy object, which police have yet to find.

According to police, Mr. Bede found his wife in the front parlor and called for both police and an ambulance. Mrs. Bede was dead by the time the ambulance arrived.

A week later, state police charged Bede with the murder and he was held on $500,000 bail at the Windham County Jail.

He was released after posting bond and was awaiting trial when the surprise announcement came from Attorney General William Houser late Tuesday afternoon.

The announcement was brief, saying only that all charges were being dropped due to lack of evidence.

Chief State Police Investigator G. William Riley, said later that he was mystified by the decision. "We brought them a strong case," he said. "I'll be talking to the attorney general in the morning."

Bede, contacted at home, said he was much relieved. "I did not kill my wife." he said, "She was a fine and wonderful woman and mother. We'd never spoken a harsh word to each other in the ten years we were married.

I have no idea what led the police to believe I could have done such a thing."

Mr. Bede holds over 500 patents and is well-known from coast to coast for his work. He holds two degrees from M.I.T., a B.S. and a Ph.D., and a law degree from Harvard.

"There was no sign of forced entry or even a struggle," Riley said. "Nor was anything missing, and that's what led us to Bede. The coroner's report also made it clear that Mrs. Bede had not been sexually assaulted. We found no evidence that anyone outside the family had been in the house."

Bede, when told what Riley had said Tuesday afternoon, said it was a "ridiculous comment. Of course there was no sign of forced entry. We live in the country. We have never locked our doors, even at night. This is another example of shoddy police work, as I have said from the start. In cases like this, they have a punch list that they go through and when nothing turns up they arrest the husband. I have no doubt that in this case I was arrested because I was so outspoken last year in the Miller case when the police did the very same thing. They lost that case too, again for lack of evidence, though they managed to put Hugh Miller through a six-month-long trial and destroyed his reputation in the process."

Hugh Miller was charged by Waterbury Police with murdering his wife in a fit of jealous rage, but the jury found him innocent.

Asked what he planned to do from here on, Bede said he would do what he had been doing since the day his wife was killed. He would get on with his life. "The hardest part," he said, "is trying to explain to my sons how something like this could have happened, and then to heal as many of their wounds as I can. My loss is inconsequential compared to theirs."

I sat staring at the screen, long after I'd finished reading the story. It was the saddest thing I'd ever read. I began searching for other files and I found plenty of stories about Augustus Bede, but after a brief flurry of stories following the charges having been dropped, there was only a single piece about the murder, printed some years later. It was short, only two paragraphs long, and all it said was that police, having found no new evidence, had given up their investigation into the death of Mary Bede.

I had copies made of the main stories, left the library, and walked out to the car. I had no idea where this was going, but I knew I had to learn more, though what else there was to learn beyond what I had read, I couldn't begin to say.

But I was curious ... very curious, and that has always caused trouble for cats.

THREE

Second Stringer

On Thursday I found out that I had made the team all right but I wasn't the starting second baseman. That went to Henry Dufresne who had been the shortstop the year before. One of the new guys got the shortstop job. They were both juniors. I knew I was better at second than Henry, though he was a better hitter, but the new kid, Charlie Heyman, was a terrific hitter.

To say I was discouraged didn't cover half of what I felt. Dad was the first to notice me moping around, as if the world had come to an end.

"What's wrong, Nick?" he asked as I finished loading the dishwasher, another one of my jobs.

I told him and I got no sympathy.

"You made the team, didn't you?"

"I'm better at second than Henry," I said.

"Then why did Coach put Henry there?"

I hate having to admit to what's true in a situation like that, because once you admit it, it's hard to justify being angry. But there wasn't much choice. "He's a little better hitter, I guess."

"Well, then you know what to do. Make yourself a better hitter."

"At batting practice you get only about ten hits each day. It's not enough. And by the time I drive down to the batting cages it costs me a whole week's allowance."

"Is there another way to improve?"

"What I need is my own batting cage."

"And how much would that cost?"

"A lot. Three thousand."

"You can't be serious."

"I asked Coach."

"Well, then you'll just have to make the most of batting practice and if it costs you your allowance to use the batting cages, maybe that's the price you'll have to pay."

"If I didn't have to pay for the gas, I'd be able to hit more."

And then he took me by surprise. "Okay. I guess I can cover that. It's not like you're wasting the money, after all. Cost of education."

It picked me up considerably. "All right, Dad! Thanks!"

He grinned. "Maybe you can make it up by raising your grades. There's no reason why you can't make honors."

Parents don't understand the social structure of high schools. They don't know that the people who get high grades are geeks or nerds and live at the bottom of the food chain.

"Let me explain something, Nick," he said. "Once you

start to get good grades, the teachers begin to think about you differently. It opens doors. And by learning how to work every day, when you get to the SATs you'll do a whole lot better. And don't think I don't know about how the cool people don't have high grades. What do you think we went through with Beth? Same old, same old."

"She got into college."

"Sure, but if she'd worked a little harder she could've gotten into a better college. It's hard to understand now, but you have think about the future, the future six years from now when you graduate from college. Today is when you lay the groundwork for that."

"Okay," I said, "I'll do my best."

I'm sorry to say I didn't mean it. My plan was to look like I was working hard and then blame it on my teachers when I didn't make honors. Okay, so it was a dumb plan, but it was all I could think of. I hate getting cornered.

To show him I meant business, though, I went right up to my room after I'd finished the dishwasher, and I left my door open so they could see I was working. I got out my history book, opened it to the chapter I'd been assigned and began reading. And something happened. I don't know what. I have no idea how or why, but I read all the way through the chapter without once losing my train of thought. I even answered the questions at the end with no problem because I remembered what I had read.

I gotta tell you. That was weird. I hate history. I have always said I hated history. It's boring. History teachers are so boring they should be bottled and sold to replace sleeping pills. Or maybe someone could tape their lectures so you could play them when you can't fall asleep. But on that Thursday night, reading about the beginning of World War I in Europe, I was not bored. And because I was pretty sure we'd have a surprise quiz on the reading, I read it a second time and took a few notes on what I thought was important.

Even after all that work I had plenty of time to read the short story for English, get my geometry done (easy), and Spanish and, finally, to tackle biology. That took me a little longer, but science usually did. Even so, when I looked up it was ten-thirty, and I had finished every bit of homework.

I thought I must be coming down with something. How else could I explain what had happened? Not only that but I wasn't even tired. I brushed my teeth, said good night, shut off my lights, and closed the door. Standard routine. I re-aimed the telescope and got ready to home in on Mr. Bede. But the house was dark. There were no lights anywhere. I could not remember the house being dark, but then I hadn't been watching all that long. Maybe he'd just gone to bed early. Or maybe he was in a room on the other side of the house with the door closed.

I sat back away from the scope, looking absently up toward the hill. The night was dark, with no moon, but because the house sat up so high, everything was silhouetted against the sky behind. And then I saw something move and I focused the telescope. It was a man, Mr. Bede, kneeling on the ground in the old family graveyard out behind the barn. He knelt with his head down as if he were praying and he was very still. I could feel a lump come up in my throat as I watched. Poor old guy, I thought, all alone, his boys gone, his wife dead. It made my trouble with second base seem pretty small. In fact it made all the stuff I worried about seem like nothing.

I decided not to watch. It was private and nobody should be watching someone at a time like that. I was putting the cap back on the lens of the telescope when I saw him stand and walk away. He limped, favoring his right leg the way Grandpa Rivers does when he gets up after he's been sitting for awhile, but he didn't walk toward the house. Instead he walked off to the east, disappearing slowly one step at a time down behind the hill. What's wrong with this picture? I asked. What's on the other side of the hill? I couldn't remember and I vowed that tomorrow on the school bus I'd be sure to sit on that side so I could see what was there.

I forgot, of course, and I never even remembered I'd forgotten until I went to lunch. I'd have to wait till Monday. Mom was picking me up from baseball practice and from the car I wouldn't be high enough to see over the rise.

Paul and Ronnie set their trays on the table and sat down. "That history quiz sucked," Paul said.

"I hope he drops the lowest grade," Ronnie said.

And when I said nothing they stared at me. "I thought it was pretty easy," I said and shrugged.

They looked at me as if they'd discovered maggots in their lunch.

"All you had to do was read it and answer the questions," I said.

"You read it?" Paul was astonished. "I mean, you actually read history! Nobody reads that stuff! It's too dangerous. Anything that boring will turn your eyes to stone."

I shrugged again. "Weird, huh? I actually thought it was

pretty interesting. I never knew much about World War I."

"But who cares?" Ronnie asked. "I mean, like, who could possibly care what happened all those years ago? It's all gone by. It's dead."

I shrugged yet again. "Must've been something I ate."

"You know what I heard," Paul said. "I heard that no cheerleader ever dates a guy who makes the honor roll."

My mouth went to work before my brain cut in or I would never have said what I did. "They're all airheads."

You'd have thought I had sworn in church.

"The boy has lost it entirely," Ronnie said. "Maybe we should take him down to the nurse."

"I'm thinking nine-one-one," Paul said.

We all laughed and then the subject switched to other things and we were back to being old buds again. But we didn't laugh too loud or carry on too much. We were, after all, just sophomores, and though that's better than being a freshman (freshmen are all short and scared), it wasn't a whole lot better because sophomores have more pimples. Pimples. Don't get me started. Nevermind. I'm started. Pimples. They were invented to make sure you don't grow up too fast. Here's the way it works. The instant your face clears up a little, you begin to feel pretty good about yourself, even a little confident, maybe even confident enough to ask someone out. The next day you wake up and there's some gigantic oozing whitehead, or worse, whole outcroppings on your chin and your nose and all you want to do is wear a bag over your head for the rest of the day. A bad hair day is one thing, but a bad pimple day comes as close as you can get to the end of life on Earth as we know it.

From then on all you can do is wait and wait, but even knowing that it will pass, that one day your face will decide all on its own to go out of the pimple farming business, makes it not one jot easier. (See that word? Jot? I picked it up from reading mysteries written by English writers.)

"Hey, Paul" I said. "I've got a question. Your grandparents live in town, right?"

"Now there's a weird question," Paul said.

Ronnie nodded. "Good ol' Nick, the master of the weird question." He bit into his sandwich. "I think I know where this is leading. More info on good ol' Mr. Bede, right?"

"Yeah, right."

"What's that all about?" Paul asked.

"Do you know the story about how someone murdered his wife?" I asked

"Everybody knows that story."

"But nobody ever found the murderer."

"Mom says that's 'cause he got away with it," Paul said.

"He didn't do it," I said. "The attorney general threw the case out for lack of evidence."

"My mother says he paid everybody off," Paul said. "He's really rich, you know."

"Maybe you oughta explain to your mother how you're innocent until you're proven guilty in court," I said.

Paul grinned. "With my mother everybody is guilty all of the time, every part of every day."

"Except Mr. Bede," I said.

"How do you know that?"

"Because last Saturday I went over to UConn and looked it all up in the library." It was a stunner, and I really, really wished I hadn't said it because it didn't take my wise-ass friends long to react.

"Whattya think, Paul," Ronnie said, "is it time to change tables?"

"Absolutely. No way can we be seen sitting with a guy who went to a library on a Saturday."

"You think maybe there's some kind of virus loose, like maybe some geek virus?" Ronnie asked.

"What else could it be? I mean you can never tell what you'll pick up in libraries."

"But he must've had it before he went, or ..."

"All right. All right. Ease up. I'm trying to be serious here. I need to find somebody in town who knew him when it happened. Maybe somebody he went to school with. You got any suggestions?"

Paul shrugged. "All four of my grandparents and probably Ronnie's too. They're all about the same age."

"Would they talk to me?"

Ronnie laughed. "The problem will be getting them to shut up once they get started."

"Okay. Who's first?"

"I'll ask Grandpa Jones," Paul said. "He loves to talk about old times." He shook his head. "I'll call you later."

"Good."

'Still," Ronnie said, "you're worrying me. You get onto something, Nick, and you never know when to quit. Take your bounce-back pit, for example."

"It worked, didn't it?"

"Okay, you made the team, but you're not starting."

"Neither is any sophomore, and only one other made the

team. I'm thinking I need a batting cage."

"Whoa, cool," Paul said. "Those things are awesome!"

"You're serious, right?" Ronnie asked. "A batting cage? You'd need a thousand bucks!"

"Three grand," I said, "but half of that is for the net and the frame. I got an idea how to get around that."

"Like what?"

"I have to check some web sites."

☞　　☞　　☞

Baseball practice. Of all the things there are to do I like baseball practice best. Maybe it's the time of year, spring, with the grass getting green, or the way the voices seem to float in the cool air or the crack of the bat or the feel of a ground ball coming up into my glove just right, but whatever it is, I like it.

And that day I liked it better than ever because I fielded every ground ball perfectly and every throw to first was dead nuts on. I made the turn on the double play and my throw was straight and strong. I was the only infielder who was even close to perfect, and the new hotshot shortstop couldn't make a throw from the hole, and he never once touched the bag making the double play, and he wasn't so hot on ordinary ground balls either.

Henry also did not have a good day. He was used to shortstop where the ball comes at you with a true spin. At second nearly everything is squibbed and spinning as much sideways as end over end, so you gotta have a very quick glove, allowing you to adjust at the last second.

Not that Henry wasn't a good fielder, because he was ... when he played short and had longer to look at the ball. But the new guy could flat-out hit. He was over six feet tall and he had broad shoulders and he hit monster line drives, even when Coach was pitching.

While I waited in the on deck circle, I watched him swing, paying close attention to the way he timed each pitch and how he was ready to hit each pitch. Anything close to the plate, he got a piece of it, either smacking it into the outfield or fouling it off. How many times had I heard it? How many times had I read it? Take what the game gives you. Six miserable words. Nothing to it, right? Guess again.

But I came up to the plate determined to try, determined not to swing at any bad pitches. All I wanted was to get a good look and go to the opposite field because that gave me more time to see the ball.

So, of course, every pitch I saw was on the inside of the plate, just off the edge. I fought them off, fouling everything until I got one pitch out over the plate and hit it to right field; a soft fly ball, easily caught. It was pretty disappointing, I gotta tell you. Only the last one was any good. A bunt. Everybody was supposed to bunt on the last pitch, but I never showed bunt until the pitch was almost there and then I let my bat fall into the pitch and dumped it down the third base line and beat the throw to first by a mile.

Coach never said a word, and I grabbed my hat and glove and trotted out to second. What I needed was my own batting cage.

FOUR

Bede's Story

Sunday afternoon Paul took me to meet his grandfather. If I'd been going to meet an ordinary adult, I'd have been a little nervous but grandparents aren't like parents. They don't think they have to act like the big dog all the time.

Paul's grandfather, Mr. Jones, was a man of medium height, mostly bald but for a fringe of snow white hair over his ears and around the back of his head. He had blue eyes and when he smiled his face cracked into thousands of lines that made you smile back. Despite his large stomach he moved around easily enough and best of all, he liked to laugh.

"So," he said, as he settled into his favorite chair, one of those loungers that have an automatic footstool, "you want to know about Augie Bede ... now what brought that up?"

"He's my neighbor but nobody on our road knows anything about him. All the houses except his are new and everybody who lives there is new in town, so that might explain why nobody knows him, but he also keeps to himself pretty much and I guess some people worry about that, especially since he lives alone too."

He grinned. "You've been talking to Ronnie's mother."

I nodded.

"Well, never mind that," He shook his head. "I haven't heard anyone mention Augie for years. It's almost like he was already dead. Funny how a thing like that happens." He crossed his legs at the ankles. "Augie and I are the same age, eighty-six. We went to the same school, we were in the same class, and we were even pretty good friends, or at least as good a friend as Augie allowed. It wasn't that he was unfriendly, just smart, terribly smart. And because of that he was always thinking about things, and once he got started it was like the rest of the world just went away. But that was Augie. It was just the way he was and nobody made anything of it. He didn't play sports. He read all the books in the library by the time he was ten, and he was always way, way ahead of our teachers.

"But if you talked to him he always had a ready smile and he was perfectly friendly. When all of us started to grow, he grew like a weed. I think he finally got to six-eight and he was so skinny when he turned sideways in the woods, you couldn't see him." Mr. Jones chuckled and his belly shook like that Santa Claus poem. "He was built like a scarecrow and that's why some of the kids used to call him Crow. I never knew whether he liked the name or not, but he answered to it. Come to think of it, though, I never called him that. He was Augie and that's what I always called him. But the other guys called him Crow. We were a tight knit little group for most of high school." He smiled at the memory. "There was me and Augie and Warren Gagne and Kenny Blaise and Willy Booth. Oh, we had some wild times, we did, though most of the wild stuff didn't include Augie. Not because we didn't want him there, but because he was too busy working in the shop his father had built in the barn. Had heat and everything. The two of them spent countless hours out there tinkering. They built some pretty strange stuff, I can tell you. Most of the time we had no idea what it was. Now that I think back on it, I'm surprised we weren't more curious. I don't even remember asking about it.

"But Augie, well, Augie, he could fix anything. Anytime anyone had trouble with their car they took it to Augie. Not only did he do it for nothing, but he was better than any of the local mechanics. He'd stand there listening to the engine and taking it apart in his mind. I remember one time Pete Johnson brought his pickup over. He said it wasn't running right and sometimes it made a whirring sound at forty.

"Augie listened to the engine and he had Pete rev it up and then he took it for a drive and when they came back Augie got out his tools and began taking things apart from the top of the engine down. After he got the camshaft exposed, he took out a calipers and began measuring. It was out of round, he said. So Pete ordered a new camshaft and put it in and the sound disappeared.

"He was always doing favors like that for everybody, and in those days this was a small town with nothing but farms, and in a place like that when someone does you a favor, you do them one. Augie had us keep our eyes peeled for all sorts of junk metal and engines. We kept him well supplied. I think some of that stuff is probably still sitting either in his front yard or in the barn. And he always had a dozen car engines that he was working on, though just what he did to them he never said.

"And he was expert at getting people to do stuff for him. He had no metal working machinery, no lathes, nor millers, but he made a deal with Karl Swenson who owned a machine shop over in Burrilville, that he'd work for nothing if he could do some machining on his own on the weekends.

"He was so good that Mr. Swenson paid him anyway, and the story that went around said that Augie had made so many improvements in the shop that Karl was delighted to pay him and let him use the machinery anytime he wanted just for being there. That lasted a year and then his father bought a lathe and a miller and a big press and a drill press and metal bending machinery and all kinds of other machines. The shop got so big it took up half the barn."

He looked up. "You know, I could use a cup of coffee."

"I'll get it, Gramps," Ronnie said.

"Get yourselves a couple of sodas while you're at it. There's Pepsi in the fridge."

Ronnie came back with the coffee and handed it to his grandfather and then brought the sodas.

Mr. Jones took a sip and looked over the rim of his cup at me. "But I'm going to guess here, that what you're most interested in is the murder, is that right?"

I nodded. "I went over to UConn and looked it up in the old newspapers."

"And what did you think?"

"About the murder?"

He nodded.

"I don't think he killed his wife," I said.

"Right you are." He shook his head. "Nobody with any sense could have believed that, and certainly no one who knew him did. But a whole lot of people in this town thought differently and still do. It raised quite a ruckus. There's still people who won't talk to each other, but I'll get to that later."

He set his cup down, sat quietly for several seconds and then began again. "After we graduated from high school most of us got jobs and some went off to college. Augie went to M.I.T. up in Boston, but that didn't mean much to us then. The only colleges we heard about had good football, hockey, or basketball teams.

"Summers he came home, and we all got together now and then, but it's never quite the same after high school is over. I went to work on the farm with my Dad, Kenny went into the insurance business with his father, Warren went off to college to become a teacher, and Willy ... now that's a sad story. He went to work in the woolen mill learning to be a weaver. One day, on a Saturday morning, he and his younger brother, Gordon, were hit sideways by a truck. It crushed the car, killing Willy instantly. His little brother, who was seven years younger, survived but he got pretty banged up. He was never quite right after that." He shook his head. "Terrible tragedy. They were a good strong family and they pulled together. Had a big farm and there were two older brothers and Gordon ended up working on the farm till he died. He was only forty or so. Just went to bed one night and didn't wake up in the morning. A stroke, the doctors said, the result of the head injury from the accident. Most of the farm was sold several years ago for house lots, like so many other farms, and they all still live there in houses they built."

"What did Mr. Bede's father do?" I asked.

"He worked for Pratt and Whitney Aircraft. Everyone said he had a very good job in engineering. He was the only boy in the family and he got the house and farm when his parents died and he moved in and rented out the land. He had one sister, older. She married Clayton Gangler and they moved off West somewhere. Oregon, I think.

"Augie had a sister too, Pearl, much older. She went to college, got married, and went to live in Boston. Augie just kept going to school. At first we thought maybe he wasn't so smart because it was taking him so long to finish. Then one day we read in the paper how he had earned his Ph.D. in physics at M.I.T. and had started law school at Harvard.

"And then one day he was back home. His parents were quite old by then, and his father died a couple of years later and then his mother took ill and Augie just stayed on and he didn't seem to have any kind of a job and people thought he must have been left something by his father. But the truth came out when there was another story in the newspapers about how he had been granted three patents. You could have knocked us over with a straw. Those three new patents put him over a hundred patents and he wasn't yet thirty!

"About a year later his mother passed on and still nothing changed, at least at first. Then we heard that he had been seen at a restaurant with Mary Packard. She was ten years younger and she was something of a looker. She'd just graduated from college in Massachusetts and the next thing we knew they were married. Who would have thought a girl as pretty as Mary Packard would find anything the least attractive in Augustus Bede the Fourth? Tall, skinny, with a long face and shaggy hair and rumpled clothes, he wasn't anyone's idea of a catch. But he had very kind blue eyes and while he was a little distant, there wasn't anyone in town had anything bad to say about Augie Bede, especially after he came home and took care of his parents the way he did. People here value folks who live up to their responsibilities.

"At first, after they were married, Augie and Mary traveled a good deal. They went to England and France and Italy and Sweden, and even to Japan, and all over the U.S. Then she got pregnant and they had two boys, one after another, and they settled down and began raising their family.

"Mary was always active in town, especially in the church and the schools, and when the boys were both in school, she got a job as a teacher and everyone said there was none better than Mary Packard Bede.

"They just became part of the town as their families had before them. Augie was seen now and again in passing, much the way any of us saw each other. He was always humble and friendly and always willing to help, if the need arose. His name was in the papers fairly often because of the patents he got and he traveled some on business. They were a good solid family, and we were proud to have them living among us. Truth to tell, Augie was kind of our claim to fame, especially since he'd been born here and hadn't come in from the outside.

"Then one horrible night it all flew apart. Somebody murdered poor Mary and suddenly people I'd always known began saying that it was Augie had done it. I was having none of that, I can tell you. Augie might have been eccentric and smart, and a whole lot of other things that none of us were, but that didn't make him a murderer." He frowned and rubbed his chin. "I lost my best friend over it. Kenny Blaise. He couldn't talk about it without getting red in the face like a beet. And when the attorney general dropped the charges, he was ready to lead a lynch mob. Never did anything so tear this town apart ... never! Why even the Booth family was in a uproar over it, and that made no sense to me a'tall. You'd think a family that had suffered as they had, would've been first to offer comfort to Augie, but it was almost like they were afraid they'd lose their position as the most long suffering family in town." He shook his head. "Can't think why anyone would want to be known that way, but there's no figuring some people.

"Everywhere you went there was all kinds of wild talk about how he'd bought off the law. People said it was another example of the rich always getting their way. They just wouldn't accept the fact that there was no evidence.

"It was very sad. Some families still won't have anything to do with each other." He picked up his coffee mug. "And now I'm thinking I ought to stop by and say hello. In fact, I can't think why I haven't. Pretty poor way to treat an old friend. I haven't talked to him since the troubles."

"Why would anyone have killed Mary Bede?" I asked.

"Complete mystery. The town fairly crawled with police for two years, but nothing ever surfaced, and they finally gave it up. Could have been a burglar. You know, an outsider, a complete stranger. It would have been easy enough to get in. Nobody ever locked their doors. We just never thought about it. After that we did, though." He sipped his coffee and looked directly at me. "The likelihood is that it was someone in town, someone with a reason that none of us knew about or understood. There's lots of reasons why people kill each other, and most of them seem to be common enough. But the reasons don't work until you find somebody to hang them on and the police couldn't find a soul."

"Did she have any enemies?"

"Not a one, which was part of why it split the town so. Some said it had to be an outsider because neither of them had a single enemy. Others said it was an insider and that meant it was Augie. Never understood the logic of that. But if he'd never had an enemy before, suddenly he had a lot of them, most likely the result of his success. They were envious, or they resented the way he kept to himself. They envied his money and his brilliance, even the property he had inherited. Some even said he had driven his sister off to keep her from getting the property." He shook his head. "To be sure we can never know what's inside anyone's head. It doesn't matter how well you know someone, you can never know that. So, of course any of those things people said could have been true. I just knew they weren't.

"I've met men I knew could kill and I steered far away from them. I know people in this town who could kill someone, if they felt they were justified. But I never believed Augie could kill anyone."

He took a swallow of coffee and looked off toward the far wall. "Still, there is always the chance. I mean, suppose Mary had decided to leave him? A divorce would have meant losing the farm and not seeing his sons grow up and he was very proud of his sons. It would have meant losing the only woman he had ever loved." He looked down at the coffee mug he held in his huge, gnarly old hands. "My father always said that people who seek only their own counsel are more likely to make bad decisions because they can never be smart enough to consider every possibility."

"But you still don't think he did it?" I asked.

"No, I don't, and that's a fact."

"Do you think anyone could find out who did?"

He looked at me carefully, guessing, I thought, at what I had on my mind. "It's a cold trail now."

"But not so cold if the murderer is still living here."

He grinned. "Got someone in mind?"

"No. I just thought ..."

"I understand that it might seem like a pretty exciting thing to do, trying to find the killer, but you'd best not try."

"But ..."

"Remember what I said about how it divided people in town. If anyone starts stirring into things, it will only bring up all the anger we put to bed so long ago. We didn't kill it, we only put it to sleep, and it would be quick to wake, and when something like that happens, the person who kicks the yellow jacket nest is the first to get stung."

I smiled. "I don't like yellow jackets," I said, hoping to throw him off the scent, because in fact I was going to kick that nest as hard as I could. I knew it as clearly as I knew that the sun would set in the evening and rise in the morning. The only problem was finding out which lump to kick.

FIVE

Going Batty

Saturday morning after the first week of practice, I headed down to the batting cages with Ronnie and Paul, and it was a very cool ride with Phish blasting out of the radio of my Mom's Volvo wagon, which, while it might not be a car guys our age would chose to profile in around town, being as any kind of wagon is definitely not cool, and in Volvos only a convertible has any status at all, it does have a great sound system, and that, as everyone knows, is the first thing you look for in a car. It's gotta be loud and the bass has to thunder. The Volvo sound system is pretty conservative in the matter of bass but you can crank the sound up big time. And with the sound up and windows open, people know you're making a statement.

While I headed for the batting cages, Ronnie and Paul hit the driving range. Both their dads play golf and belong to the Valley Hills Country Club. Ronnie and Paul are really into golf. So is my dad. He's a member too and I play with him now and then, but I'm awful, and he keeps thinking he's a golf coach, so mostly I only like hitting balls on the range. This year they built a range at the club but it won't be ready till the turf takes root. Golf is a nasty game and I'd decided to stick to baseball, which was giving me all the trouble I could handle. I laced up my spikes, pulled on my gloves, put on my batting helmet, and stepped into the batting cage, fully expecting to hit the hide off the ball.

No such luck. I had the slowest bat in the east. I was behind every pitch and even when I forced myself to start my swing as soon as I saw the ball, I couldn't get the bat on it. I fouled a few here and there, always to the right side, but I just could not get the bat and the ball to collide over the plate. Maybe I needed glasses or something. I went through two rounds, hacking away like a madman, vaguely aware of an older man standing outside the cage watching. I assumed he was waiting for the machine, but I had a pocket full of quarters and I wasn't quitting.

I dropped the money into the machine and got ready. Out of the corner of my eye, I saw the man leave and then saw him again when he came back carrying a bat.

I tried to focus. Maybe it was my eyes, I thought, maybe I needed glasses. One thing for sure, the more I missed, the angrier I got, and that, of course, only made it more impossible. I stopped at the end of the round to get my breath and try to calm down, and the man behind me spoke.

"Say there, young fella," he said. "I think maybe you're using too heavy a bat. What's that weigh? Thirty-four ounces? I got a bat here you're welcome to try. Twenty-eight ounces.

Should be just about right."

"No," I said, "my bat's all right." I was a little grumpy just then and my manners had slipped considerably.

"Well, you might give it a try," he said. "Can't hurt."

I looked at him carefully. He was only a little taller than I, with a definite, grandfather sort of look, and he had a pleasant smile and a relaxed way of speaking that put you at ease.

"Hitting is a matter of bat speed," he said. "The faster the bat travels, the easier it is to hit the ball."

I knew that. Of course I knew that, but I was still balky.

"I used to play, when I was younger," he said.

Never talk to strangers, right? But hey, I was sixteen and I wasn't exactly a weakling, and I had two of my buddies with me and well, sometimes you just have to listen to what someone has to say. In fact, I was desperate because if I couldn't hit better, then I was gonna ride the bench for the whole damn baseball season, and that was not an option.

"Okay," I said, "I guess I need to try something."

He laughed and handed me the bat. It was made of wood and it had a name I'd never heard of: Strike Force. I couldn't remember ever using a wooden bat. Everything is aluminum now, except for the pros. And I had to admit as I held the bat it felt comfortable, light, and the handle was very thin and easier to grip than my bat. I dropped the money into the machine and got ready, almost holding my breath as I anticipated hitting the ball. The fist pitch came in a little high, but I kept my eye on it and drove a liner straight back at the machine in a line drive. All right! Next pitch. Smokin', faster by a lot and I swung into it, my head turning with the ball as it flew into the bat. This time I hit it to center.

I won't say I hit every pitch, because I didn't, but I sure hit most of them and I had some big silly smile plastered across my face by the time the machine shut off.

"Wow! I can't believe it! I never hit like that before!" I dug into my pocket for more quarters.

"Whoa, there. Give yourself a little break. You've been hitting steadily for half an hour. Let the muscles relax a little."

I nodded, picked up my bat, stepped out of the cage, and handed him his bat. "That is an amazing bat," I said. "Thanks."

"Glad to help."

"Can I get a bat like that in aluminum?"

"Sure. But why not stay with wood?"

"Isn't aluminum better?"

"It's a matter of opinion. I like wood bats. It doesn't sound like baseball with aluminum." He grinned.

"What's special about this bat?" I asked.

"Not much except the grain in the wood." He pointed to the barrel of the bat. "See how wide the grain is? That gives you more power. The wood is ash, but not just any ash. This bat is made from northern-grown ash, which is harder."

"How do you know so much about bats?" I asked.

"Because I make 'em."

"You made this?"

"And a couple of thousand like it. I started a few years ago, but business is pretty slow so far. Wood bats break. But for what you paid for that aluminum bat you could buy four of mine and that would get you through the season. Most guys don't even break a single bat."

Something still didn't add up. "Do you come down here

to test your bats?"

"Nope. I come down here on Saturday mornings and look to see if I can't help a young fella, like yourself, who needs a bat he can hit with." He grinned. "And then I make him a present of one bat." He handed it back to me, reached into his pocket, took out a card, and handed it to me. "The next one, you have to buy, and because it's a good idea to have a spare on hand in case you break one, I recommend that you buy at least one. But that's up to you. Talk to your folks and see what they think. Try it out in practice."

"Thanks," I said. "How much are they?"

"Thirty dollars. Not cheap for a wood bat, but still cheaper than aluminum in the long run." He smiled. "Now you're thinking what kind of snake oil salesman have I run into here? And I don't blame you. But all I'm trying to do is get my bats out there so people know they have an option. I don't make this offer to everyone who turns up here, though. I look around for a guy who's got a good stroke."

That got my attention, I can tell you. "You think I can hit?"

"Sure. You've got a good clean swing. You step into the ball easily and your swing is dead level. I'm guessing you play second or maybe short, is that right?"

"How could you tell that?"

"Just a guess."

"Pretty good guess."

"I watch a lot of baseball. It's my game. And even if I don't sell a lot of bats yet, I get a big kick out of making 'em." He looked down at the bat. "Couple of other things you ought to know about my bats. Every one comes boned and I only use perfect pieces of wood."

"What's boned?"

"In the old days players used a soup shank bone, rubbing the barrel of the bat to compact the wood fibers. A friend of mine made a machine for me so I can do that automatically now. All you need is a little pine tar and you're in business. The real trick is fitting the bat to the player. Most guys want the biggest bat they can find and usually that's what keeps them from hitting."

It clicked immediately. "Somebody made a machine?"

"Sure did."

"How does it work?"

He looked at me for several seconds and then nodded his head. "It uses a series of offset hardened steel rollers under hydraulic pressure. Simple to build, simple to use. He made one for me and then sold the patent rights to Hillerich and Bradsby for a bundle. The guy's a genius."

"Augustus Bede?"

He laughed. "Pretty good guess."

"I live just down the road from him."

"Then you know him."

"He keeps pretty much to himself."

"Go say hello sometime. Most fascinating man I ever met. He'd love to show you around."

I must have looked as if I didn't believe him.

He laughed. "Yeah," he said, "most people think he's some kind of hermit, but there's no truth to that. He's just busy all the time solving problems for manufacturers all over the world. He's even got a web site." He pointed to the bat. "What do you think?"

"I never hit like this before." I glanced down at the ground. "But I don't have enough money with me to buy another bat."

"Never thought you would. You talk to your folks first. If you want a bat give me a call. I'm in Phoenixville. Not hard to find. Bring your dad along. Always like to show off my shop. But be sure to call first."

I looked down at the card. Tom Baines. "Thanks, Mr. Baines," I said. "Thanks a lot."

"Now get in there and go to work. Get that swing grooved and then switch to the machine that throws curves."

"Thanks again," I said.

"My pleasure," he said. And then he turned and walked down along the row of cages, looking for another hitter.

Back in the cage, I dug in and waited. It was like magic. Suddenly I could hit. I felt like I'd had a meeting with the genie from the magic lamp.

The curve ball machine caused a few problems at first, but in the end I hit curves as easily as fastballs and I can tell you I couldn't wait for practice on Monday. I also couldn't wait to check out Mr. Bede's web site.

When I ran out of money for the batting machine I walked over to the driving range where Paul and Ronnie were whacking away at golf balls and hitting them pretty straight.

I sat on a bench behind them, watching and thinking more and more about Mr. Bede and wondering if I could ever work up the courage to just drop in on him. At least the bat gave me an excuse. I could take it up there and show it to him. But I was pretty sure I wasn't going to do that right away. I mean, suppose he was a murderer after all? What if he *had* bought his way out of trouble? I couldn't tell my parents I was going up there, so nobody would know I was there if anything happened. Look, I know that sounds crazy, because after all, he was an old guy who limped and there was no way he could catch me, but I kept thinking about how smart he was and how a guy like that could set a trap I'd never see and the next thing you know I'd be roped to some torture rack in the basement. You read about stuff like that all the time. Remember that guy in the mid-west who killed people and ate them? He even kept pieces of them in his refrigerator to snack on when he was watching television. That was the grossest thing I ever read.

"Hey," Paul said. "Where'd you get the bat?"

"What is that, wood?" Ronnie asked.

"A guy gave it to me to try out."

"But it's wood," Ronnie said.

"It's the best bat I ever tried."

We walked back to the car. "And he's just giving them away?" Paul shook his head. "Nobody gives stuff away."

"He makes 'em," I said, "and he's trying to get people to use 'em."

"Sounds weird to me," Ronnie said. "I mean, only big companies make bats."

"I thought only bats made bats," Paul said.

We all laughed. I tucked my bats into the back of the Volvo, they stored their clubs, and we climbed into the car.

"All I know is that on Monday at practice I'm gonna hit like I never hit before, and I'm gonna be starting at second."

"Dream on, Dude," Paul said. "Sophomores never start."

"Yeah, well this one is," I said.

"I just wish we had some Jayvee teams, like at least one for golf," Ronnie said. "They only take ten guys on the team and guys like us with a ten handicap never get a chance."

"Sucks big time," Paul said.

"Why don't you try to put together a team at the Country Club?" I asked.

"You mean to play against other clubs?" Ronnie asked.

"There's gotta be other guys in the same position, right?"

"Whattya think, Paul?"

He shrugged. "Let's ask Mr. Pizzaro. Heck, we can come up with ten guys easy, and all of 'em are members."

"And we can find enough guys to drive so transportation wouldn't be a problem."

"But there is one problem," Paul said. "The same guys who beat us out this year will turn up in the summer."

"So," I jumped in, "have a spring team and a summer team and in the summer have two levels, those below a ten handicap and those above a ten handicap."

"I'm starting to like this idea a lot," Ronnie said.

"It's giving me goosebumps," Paul said.

I started the car and turned on the radio and that pretty well eliminated any conversation on the way home, and from the way people reacted in the cars next to us when we stopped at the lights, we knew we had got it just right. The parents were horrified and their kids were grooving. Parents have to learn to be a little tolerant, I mean, from the way they act, sometimes you'd think they had never been teenagers.

So I dropped off Paul and Ronnie and when I got home I showed Dad the bat and here's what I got. Are you ready for this? Good, because I wasn't.

"You're telling me the guy just gave you the bat."

"Yup."

"Nick, you must think I'm a pretty dim bulb. Nobody gives away stuff like that."

"Well, he did. He makes 'em and he wanted me to try it out and then he gave it to me."

"Are you hearing this, Elsie?" he asked my mother.

"Yes, dear."

"Well, what do you think?"

"If he says the man gave him the bat, dear, then the man must have given him the bat."

"Nobody gives away something like this. I'll bet this bat costs fifty dollars. Nobody gives valuable stuff like that away."

"Thirty," I said.

"You see what I mean? Thirty dollars. What I can't figure is how you got out of the store with it."

And that pissed me off. He was accusing me of stealing the bat. "This sucks!" I shouted. "You're saying I stole the bat, aren't you? You're accusing me of stealing and then lying about it, and that sucks big time!"

"Now hold it right there, young man. We'll have none of that attitude or language in this house, is that clear?"

Suddenly I remembered the card, and I reached into my shirt pocket, took it out, and handed it to him. "Here, call him up and ask him."

Well, that shot some holes through his story, I can tell you. Shut him up like somebody had pulled his plug.

He studied the card and I could see he was trying to make the evidence fit his version of how I had gotten the bat, but it wasn't working.

"And if I call him, what am I going to hear?"

"Call him and find out. And you know what else? He even had Mr. Bede make him a machine to harden the wood in the bats and then Mr. Bede sold the patent to Hillerich and Bradsby. Now, what do you think of that?"

Mother rolled her eyes. "Mr. Bede? How did that awful man get into this? Do you know that he murdered his wife and got away with it? Now, I ask you what sort of man is that to have living in this neighborhood? You can see what people like that come to. Just look at the junk on his lawn!"

Sometimes I think parents watch too much television. Where else could they get such whacked out ideas?

Dad picked up the bat and turned it over and over in his hands. "Pretty well made," he said. "Is it any good?"

"Better than any bat I ever tried. I hit nearly every pitch and you can see from the marks on the barrel that I hit them right on the meat of the bat."

"And he sold the patent to Hillerich and Bradsby?"

"That's what Mr. Baines told me."

"That's pretty amazing. I asked some of the guys in my department if they'd heard of Bede and they couldn't believe that I hadn't heard of him. Apparently he holds about six patents that we pay royalties on for the rights to use them. I just never knew it."

You want to get Dad calmed down, hand him something mechanical. I suppose that's true with any mechanical engineer, but I never seem to think of it when I need to. I suppose the best thing would be to carry some little mechanical toy in my pocket and when things threaten to explode I could just pull it out, wind it up, and let it run.

Mom, however, is a horse of a different color. Heck, she's even a different horse. She has about a zillion issues, but they're all weird, like having a neat front yard or making sure the front door has a fresh coat of a paint or that you put your clothes in closets and drawers.

"Are you listening to me, Harold?"

"Yes, dear," he said, but he was still concentrating on the bat. "He must turn them on a lathe and then sand them down. That must be a pretty neat machine. Allows him to get the bat smooth without throwing it out of round."

"Sometimes I think I'm talking to the walls in this house," Mom said.

"Yes, dear," Dad said. "And they could use a good talking to, I'm sure."

"Harold!"

"What?" he looked up at her.

"Something has got to be done about Mr. Bede before he corrupts this entire neighborhood."

"Why?"

"Why? You ask why? He murdered his wife, that's why!"

But Dad was still thinking about machinery. "Maybe she deserved it," he said.

As you might guess, that wasn't the right thing to say. In fact it may have been the worst wrong thing he'd ever said.

"Deserved it? Did you say she deserved it? No wife deserves to be murdered. That is the most sexist remark I've ever heard, and to think it came from my own husband!"

Dad looked totally mystified as he glanced round at me. "What did I say?" he asked.

I shrugged. "You said maybe she deserved it," I said.

"Who deserved it? What did she deserve?"

"You haven't heard a word I said, Harold."

"Well, I was thinking about what kind of machines Mr. Baines uses and I was thinking how maybe I'd give him a call and go over and take a look at his operation. I mean, this is pretty sophisticated manufacturing and it would be interesting to see his shop."

They had been married long enough for her to know that once he was into nuts and bolts mode, she had no hope of getting through. Did I tell you that Dad is very smart? Well, he is, and that's why he's Chief Engineer at Standard Products. Mom's plenty smart too, but she gets sidetracked.

"I'm sorry, dear," he said. "You know how I get when I start thinking about something like this."

She did, and it was even part of what she liked about him. She smiled. "I just wish he'd clean up his yard."

"Who, dear?"

"Mr. Bede."

"All inventors are like that," Dad said. "They keep all sorts of junk around because they never know when they're going to need some piece of metal to machine a part from. Do you know that he holds over a thousand patents? I'd like to talk to him sometime."

"Bede? You want to talk to Bede?" She rolled her eyes.

"Yes, I would. I definitely would like to talk to Mr. Bede."

"Can I go with you?" I asked.

"I don't see why not."

"You'd risk your own son with a murderer?"

"He didn't kill her," I said. "If he had, there would've been a trial, but the attorney general dropped the charges for lack of evidence."

"Just like that movie," Dad said. " 'The Fugitive,' right?"

"Sort of," I said.

Dad picked up Mr. Baines' card. "I'll call him right now."

We spent the afternoon with Mr. Baines in the shop in his barn as he took us step-by-step through the process of making a baseball bat right from a square length of ash. It was amazing to see the bat appear from a long square piece of wood and then even more amazing to see the wood in that bat hardened in Mr. Bede's rolling machine.

Dad and Mr. Baines had a lot to talk about because as it turned out, Mr. Baines was a retired engineer and I gotta tell you that conversation got real technical in a hurry, and I wasn't sure what they were talking about most of the time. But that didn't keep me from being interested. It was a neat place and I liked watching the machinery run more than I liked my video games. Probably, as Mom would say, it was a "guy thing" but whatever it was, I liked it. In the end I came away with three more bats, all exactly like the one Mr. Baines had given me. It was a good day. But not just because I got all those new bats. Something else happened. Dad began talking to me as he never had before. Suddenly, somehow, someway I'd become one of his kind of guys. And when I suggested that maybe the two of us could build a pitching machine he got very interested.

The other thing that happened, aside from Dad nearly driving off the road twice because he was so absorbed in thinking about the pitching machine, was that I knew I was going to talk to Mr. Bede ... no matter what Mom said.

SIX

Just Another Week

Did you ever notice how some days are just not predict-
able? I have noticed this. I have also noticed that most of the
time days like that don't turn out for the better. I'm not talking here about being able to predict what's gonna happen in
any given day, because that's impossible, and even if you
could do it, things would get kind of boring.

Monday was definitely not boring. First period I got back
my English test. C. I thought I'd studied for it, so getting a C
was pretty disappointing. I don't know how things work
around your house, but grades like that in mine call for eva-
sive action, which is easier said than done. Mom is nosey.
She calls the school on the homework hotline and finds out
when tests are scheduled and what's been assigned. That
eliminates the best tactic which is simply not to tell your
parents when there's a test coming up. That way if you get a
good grade you reap the praise while you keep quiet about

the stuff you screw up. But once they know about it, they're going to ask, and I don't know about you, but with stuff like that, lying is stupid. You'll get caught and then you've got to face two penalties.

It took me a while to work out a strategy, but here's what I do. I tell them I got a C. Then I take the blame. Something along the lines of ... "I just didn't study hard enough. I mean, I thought I had, but I think I need some help in learning how to study better." The worst you have to put up with is some lecturing on how to study. But what I'm gonna tell you next ... well if you ever tell anyone I said it, I'll come looking for you, okay? The one thing you never want to admit is that anything your parents told you works.

I'm jumping ahead a little here, because I haven't told you about what happened on Monday night when Mom gave me my first lesson in how to study for the biology test I had coming up on Tuesday. I got an A on the test. What she told me worked. I won't say it was easy, because I had to outline two whole chapters and then go back over it three times, but when I sat down to take the test, it was almost easy.

Second period on Monday we got assigned an essay in history. I like to write, so that was okay, but the problem with writing essays is that the teachers keep changing their minds about how you write an essay. To tell you the truth I don't think they even know what an essay is.

Third period I have gym. There may be a bigger waste of time in school than gym, but I can't think what it might be. We had to play some dumb game, I never caught the name, but because it was a co-ed gym class we had girls on our teams and whenever that happens the gym teachers give you a whole special set of rules to make it easier for the girls. The only good part of that is that it takes them so long to explain all the dumb rules that you don't have much time to play the dumb game.

Fourth period was biology where Mrs. Wicker told us about the test the next day. Enough said.

Lunch sucked. The food was okay, but I was late getting there and I wound up sitting at a table with six girls in my class and it must have been bitch week because all they did was make nasty remarks which made me want to punch them out, which of course you can't do, because they're girls. If any guy had mouthed off the way they did, I'd have stuffed him. But not in school. You never stuff anyone in school. You wait till later when you're not on school grounds. And, to tell the truth, if it was Mike Oliver or his buddy Hamm, I wouldn't have stuffed them because I'd have wound up as the stuffing. They are both very big and strong and very nasty. Everyone's afraid of them, even the guys on the hockey team, and it takes a lot to scare those guys.

I think something has to be done about the girls. They can say anything they want to and if you come back at 'em they run to some teacher and say you were using sexist language and then you get to have a friendly little chat with the disciplinarian who in our school is a big fat gay woman who hates men. You can guess how many guys win there.

The first good thing to happen was that after lunch Cindy Bonney came up and apologized for what happened at lunch. That sure made me feel a whole lot better, but then too, Cindy and I have been friends since the first grade. I knew that because she always used to punch me in the arm and tease me. At least she hadn't punched me in a long while and, in fact, she hadn't been much a part of what went on at lunch either. And for a minute I was tempted to try and get something going with her. I mean, she is, after all, one of the prettiest girls in school and most of the time she's really nice. She likes to laugh and she's one of the smartest kids in our class. In fact, there's not much wrong with Cindy.

"Are you going to the dance next Friday?" she asked.

"I don't know."

"You ought to go."

"Are you going?" I asked.

She laughed. "Why do you think I asked if you were?"

Okay, so boys are slow about some things, and that includes me, because I sure didn't see that coming. I gotta tell you, Cindy has a smile that would melt a ski slope. She has long blond hair and blue eyes and dimples and she is thin and tall and ... well you get the picture. "I think maybe, in that case, I'll go to the dance." And then I stuck my neck out. I knew better than this, but I just couldn't help it. "Do you have a ride?" I asked.

"Jen's Mom is driving us," she said.

Maybe it was wishful thinking, but I thought I detected just the least disappointment in her voice.

"That's okay," I said. "I'll see you at the dance." I grinned. "Heck, I'll even ask you to dance."

She laughed and punched me in the arm. Hey, it was like old times.

Unfortunately, so was baseball practice. I was my usual brilliant self at second base, getting to every ball in range and some that weren't, turning the double play, and firing on to first with enough on the ball to get the runner every time. Just a normal day.

Then it came my turn to hit and I pulled on my batting gloves and walked to the plate carrying my new bat. Here it was, the acid test. I took a few practice swings, slow at first and then by the third swing getting up to speed. You could hear the bat whistle in the air and I had never been able to get my aluminum bat to sing like that.

Will Ackerman was throwing batting practice just then and he had a good live fastball and a curve which he used more as a changeup than a curve, to keep you from sitting on his fastball. But he knew I couldn't hit and he reared back and came with the heat and I came with my new bat, and because I could swing it so much faster, I hit the ball dead center and sent a long line drive up the alley in left center.

I loved it! Will tried not to show his surprise, but you could see I had gotten his attention. Not that he was about to change. We're talking nose-to-nose here. Pure macho. I had never hit his heat before and there was no way he was gonna let me hit it now. And he wasn't trying to be subtle either. He made no attempt to hit the corners or go low or high, he came right over the top, down the middle, belt high, and I smashed it down the left field line past the third baseman.

For those of you who don't know much about baseball, when you pull a fastball like that, it means there is no way he is fast enough to get that pitch past you. Most guys would have hit it to right field, or maybe the good hitters would have gotten it to center. But when you pull it, you send a signal that says you own the pitcher and that makes pitchers very uneasy. In fact, it pisses them off.

I stepped out of the box, scooped a little dirt into my hands and then dusted it off and ground my hands into the handle of the bat. It was like somebody had handed me a magic wand. All I had to do was wave it and I became something I hadn't been since Little League, a hitter. Out of the corner of my eye, I spotted Coach sitting on the bench, where he usually sat during batting practice, watching each hitter and making notes about what we were doing wrong.

I stepped back in and Will cranked into his motion. More heat, but now he tried the outside corner. The ball came in, just off the corner, but too close to take and I shot a liner over first base and into right field. It was too much and the next pitch came right at my head. I dropped under it and stood back up, refusing to move my feet.

Will was hot, you could almost see steam coming from under his cap. No way was this sophomore gonna see anything more to hit. He was too young to hit a senior pitcher. He wasn't big enough or strong enough. But the fact that I had hit every pitch he'd put near the plate also meant he was gonna have to shift gears, because now he was beginning to worry that maybe he couldn't get it past me.

So he came with a curve. If I had thought about it, I'd have guessed he'd throw a curve to get me off stride, but I was focused beyond thought. I was locked onto the ball and when I saw it in his hand there was a lot of white showing and my mind recalculated automatically for a curve. Still, it was a good thing I'd spent time on Saturday hitting curves.

Curve balls don't curve unless they are thrown sidearm. Otherwise, they drop and they're slow, which means, after seeing a lot of fastballs, you're gonna swing too soon. Not today, baby. No sir. I was on it, adjusting to the drop, and I smacked a liner right back up the middle and into center.

Of course I didn't hit every pitch. I missed one, a high fastball just above the letters that was rising as it came in and I swung under it. Okay, I had a weak spot, but I could work on that; make myself lay off that pitch. No sweat. I walked back to the bench, stripping off my batting gloves and waiting for Coach to say something because there was no way he could not say something, except that he didn't say anything until I had stuffed the gloves into my back pockets and walked past him to put my bat into my own bat bag. I didn't want it in with the other bats where it might get nicked.

"New bat?"

"Got it Saturday," I said.

"Strike Force?"

I nodded.

"Tom makes a great bat."

I grinned. "Sure helped my hitting."

I really, truly, honestly expected him to offer some kind of compliment or at least some recognition that, in fact, I had just hit the hide off the ball, but all he did was nod. I got my glove and trotted back out toward second, and then on a whim I trotted over to short. Charlie was next on deck and usually Henry took over short, but today I did, for no good reason that I could think of, beyond curiosity.

"Hey," Henry called. "You think you're a shortstop?"

I grinned around at him. "You ready for the double?"

"Any time you are, dude."

The first chance I had, the ball was well to the right in the hole and I got to it on two hops, set my right leg and fired across the diamond to Jack Brodeur at first. I've always had a strong arm and the ball smacked into his mitt.

Two swings later the batter hit a grounder to second and Henry came up with it, turned and fired it to me as I came across the bag, dragging my right foot to get the force out, and then smokin' a liner to first. It felt really, really good. Almost easy. Natural.

We changed pitchers and Bobby Stallman came out to the mound. He was the other sophomore and he could throw. But he didn't have a real heater yet, because he wasn't big enough or strong enough. That would come, but for now he concentrated on accuracy, placing the ball on the inside corner, then the outside, then up, then down. Very methodical.

He produced a lot of ground balls and I got a pile of chances at short. Oddly, the balls to either side were no problem, but I had to learn to charge the grounders that came at me, making sure I controlled the hop by getting my feet into the right rhythm so that the ball didn't end up playing me. I did okay. I mean, I never missed one, but I was a little shaky a couple of times and only the quick glove I'd developed by using the bounce back saved me.

So, all in all, it was a great practice, right? Wrong. I expected Coach to say something. I mean, I had hit the ball well and I had demonstrated that I could play two positions. What more could you ask? Nothing. Not a word. And I was in a funk when Mom picked me up after practice.

I threw my backpack and the rest of my gear into the back of the Volvo, slammed the door, and climbed in.

"Bad day?" she asked.

"Yeah."

"What happened?"

"Oh, I don't know. A lot of different things."

"Oh well, it happens to us all, you know."

I knew she was right. Everybody has bad days. I just didn't want to hear about it. But Mom wasn't letting go until I cheered up a little.

"Did the new bat work okay?"

That helped. "I never hit so good before."

"Well ..."

"What?"

"You hit well."

"Right. Well. I nailed all but one pitch."

She pulled out onto the road. "What did the coach say?"

"Nothing. Absolutely nothing. He could have at least said something. All he said was something about Tom making good bats."

"Was that unusual?"

"What?"

"Does he usually go around heaping praise on people?"

I hadn't thought of that, but the instant she asked the question I realized that he never had anything good to say about anyone. I felt a lot better. I even managed a smile. "Now that you mention it, he doesn't. I mean, even when somebody makes a really great play, all he does is nod."

"Well, there you have it then. You'll just have to wait and see what happens."

The ugliest word in the English language is "wait!" All I ever did was wait. It turns up constantly in nasty sentences like: "Just wait, you'll grow out of it." The fact that it's true is no help whatsoever. Waiting sucks. What I had wanted was for Coach to come up to me and praise my hitting and tell me I was starting at second, which had been totally unrealistic. He'd wait and see how I did tomorrow and then another tomorrow and maybe a whole week, maybe even two.

"You're right," I said. "I wasn't thinking clearly." I could hardly believe I had said that. I'd admitted Mom was right and like I said, you never admit things like that. You start telling your parents they're right and it encourages them, and you can look forward to an extra dose of lectures and expectations. I could only hope she hadn't heard me.

Fat chance. She looked like she'd just won on Jeopardy.

"How'd you do on your English test?"

"I got a C. I thought I'd studied enough, but I guess I didn't. Nobody teaches you how to study."

"Now that's something I can help you with. Let's see, you have a biology test tomorrow, right? Well, after supper we'll sit down with the book and I'll show you how to comb it for the facts that will be on the test. Once you learn how to do that, your grades will go up."

There was nothing I could say. Of course, I could've said there was no need, that I had it under control, but in fact, I didn't, and in the end, I'm not dumb. If there's a better way to do things, I'm all for learning it.

The next day, when I waltzed through the bio test, I knew there was a better way. Later that week I applied the same technique to math, along with yet another technique that Dad taught me. I spent most of my time studying my old quizzes, redoing every problem I had gotten wrong until I could do them right and understand how to do them. Another A. Stuff like that is habit forming.

All that week I played ball, studied, and watched Mr. Bede. He seemed particularly busy, working late into the night and once or twice he turned on the outside lights and went out to the barn and came back carrying some chunk of metal. Each time I watched him walk out to the barn and back, thinking that something had changed, but I couldn't figure out what.

Not till Thursday night did I recognize it. He wasn't limping. In fact he almost ran sometimes. Not that there was anything so odd about that, because all old people limp sometimes. They get arthritis and some days they limp and some days they don't. The weather that week was dry and warm and I remember my grandparents never limped when the weather was like that. Sometimes the simplest explanations are the best, though I felt a little disappointed because I thought I had unearthed some major piece of information.

The other thing that happened that week was a major pimple watch. With a dance on Friday, the zit scan was in full force. I checked in the morning and then at school about a zillion times. So did every other guy in school, I think. The line stood five deep at the mirrors in the boy's room between classes.

The thing about zits is that one second you can be absolutely clear and the next time you look, bingo, there's a fat, ugly pus ball growing like a volcano in some vital place like the end of your nose or the middle of your forehead, and there's nothing you can do about it except try to cover it with makeup. Yeah, right. No way do I use makeup.

But by Thursday night, after I had closed down my Bede watch, I was still clear. By morning I was afraid to get out of bed and look in the mirror. I'd like to get hold of whoever predestined teenagers to suffer through such horror. It's not like we don't have enough to suffer through. Girls alone cause more stress than walking though a mine field.

I lay there with the covers pulled tight to my chin, knowing that I had to get up or I'd be late and I'd already had too many lates because of the mornings Mom drove me. She never gets anywhere on time.

Okay, I said to myself, how bad can it be? Are we talking one pimple, one single miserable zit, or are we talking something resembling a mushroom farm? I took a deep breath, threw back the covers, raced into the bathroom, and stared full face into the mirror. Whoa! Nothing! Absolutely clear! Not a single ... no there, just off the corner of the nose ... a red spot. A zit in the making.

I slipped in closer to the mirror, pulled a small magnifying glass from the drawer, and assessed the damage. It still had a way to go. It looked like a twenty-four hour eruption, which meant that I could put some pimple killer on it and probably get through tonight unless something happened to pressurize my system. That would shorten the time by half. Okay, the plan was clear. A total laid-back day. No pressure, just an easy glide. No matter what happens, go with the flow.

SEVEN

Go With The Flow

Go with the flow. I was the most relaxed dude in the whole school. All I did was smile and agree with everyone and at eleven-twenty Miss Foster, my art teacher, sent me to the office with a sealed note. I may have looked calm, cool, and collected, but my stomach was doing roll-overs and my heart was beating like I'd just run a hundred yard dash.

Miss Wortmann was waiting for me, hunched into the chair behind her desk. She had a habit of licking her lips over and over and all I could think of was Jaba the Hut warming up to snag some slimy snack. I waited while she read the note, getting more and more uneasy as her eyes began to twinkle and the corners of her huge mouth began to turn upward. This was a woman who enjoyed her work.

"Well then, Rivers," she said, "what have you got to say for yourself?"

I was stumped. "About what?"

"Your behavior, of course."

"I don't know what behavior you're talking about."

"Wise guys like you always play dumb, but I'll get the truth out of you sooner or later."

She was trying to bait me and I knew it, and the best thing to do when an adult does that, is to shut up.

"Miss Foster says you were acting like you're on drugs. I don't suppose you're stupid enough to have any on you, but we're going to check." She picked up the phone. "Walter, could you come in here. We have to conduct a ... search."

Mr. Feld, her assistant, was there in seconds. He looked like a nasty cat, eyes narrowed to slits, ready to pounce. "Well, well, well," he said as he rubbed his hands together. "What have we got here?"

Miss Wortmann asked me to empty my pockets while Mr. Feld went through my backpack. What they found was absolutely nothing and they were highly disappointed.

Wortmann sat behind her desk. "Okay, Walter, you can go," she said. Then she started in on me. "I know you were doing some kind of drugs, Rivers. Maybe some weed or maybe you took some Ritalin or perhaps some Valium you got from some other kid. What I want to know is who you got it from."

Here is what I know about Miss Wortmann. She is gay and she hangs out with Miss Foster who is a former nun. Now, Miss Foster is a thin, very nervous woman, always jumping around like someone's poking her with a cattle prod. There had been rumors about her, and one of those rumors said she was into downers to keep herself under control. I put the two together and decided that the best defense was a strong offense but then I chickened out. Hey, no big deal.

"We know," Miss Wortmann said "that little boys like you are very nasty. We have to watch you all the time. And when you start acting normal, we know something is up."

It took everything I had to stay calm. Little boys! Man, I could have bitten a piece out of her desk I was so mad.

"Boys do things that girls never do and they have to be reigned in all the time, especially boys who play sports. They get too wild and too full of themselves."

She leaned toward me and her breath smelled like she'd been eating dead snakes.

"The question is what sort of punishment is appropriate here. I think after-school detention for a week. That'll keep you from playing sports and get you calmed down."

She was trying to get me to flip out, trying to make me explode so she could get me expelled. And worse, I could feel that zit starting to grow. She was ruining my life and all I could do was take it. And then, out of nowhere I said, "I thought it was pretty nice of Miss Foster to give me one of her pills. It made me a lot calmer." It was a whopper of a lie and I had no idea I was going to say it until I heard myself saying it, and suddenly I felt like I was standing on the edge of a high cliff in a strong wind.

Miss Wortmann pushed back away from her desk, her eyes narrowing. "Have you told that to anyone else?"

"No." I was flying blind. I had no idea then that I had turned the tables on her. All I knew was that she had backed off and now there was no talk about detention.

"This is not something you want to talk about," she said.

I shrugged.

She began rubbing her hands together so hard I thought

she'd take off the top layer of skin. Suddenly I understood what I had done, and I felt a surge of power run through me like I had grabbed onto a hot wire. I was also so scared my knees were knocking together, because if she could prove I was lying, I would be as cooked as a missionary in a cannibal's iron pot.

"I'm going to have to look into this," she said.

I blew out of there like a rabbit running from a bad brush fire. I was in way over my head and I knew it and I also knew that I was gonna have to get a lot smarter to survive. Man, did I wish I had kept my mouth shut. But I'd been desperate. She was gonna take baseball away from me all because some nutbag teacher accused me of doing drugs, and I don't do drugs. Period. I don't do drugs because I've seen what it does to the kids who do, and I am not interested in becoming a brain-dead zombie.

On my way to lunch I stopped in the men's room for a zit progress check and it was just as I had feared. The stress had caused it to grow faster and if I didn't get things under control by tonight it would be like a big red headlight. All because of a paranoid art teacher.

I tried to imagine what she'd do next, but I couldn't seem to see that far ahead. Maybe an adult could have figured it out because they've had more experience, but all I could do was wait and see what happened.

☞   ☞   ☞

We also had our first baseball game that afternoon, a home game, but I was not in the least nervous about that, because nobody gets nervous when you know you are going to sit on the bench and there's not a chance you'll get into the game. All you do is cheer on your teammates, or maybe you get to coach first base, but I wouldn't even get to do that. Coach would use one of his seniors.

For a day in mid-April it was a nice afternoon, no wind, temperature in the sixties, couldn't have been a better day to play ball. And we drew a huge crowd of about twelve, mostly girlfriends of guys on the team, and a few parents. High school games never draw many people because they're played on weekday afternoons when everybody is working.

I sat on the bench watching Barker High score six runs in five innings while we scored nothing. Part of our problem was Heyman. He made three errors. Another part of the problem was Dufresne who still hadn't figured out how to make the turn on the double play at second, though he might have if Heyman had once given him the ball on his left side. The other part of the problem was that our pitcher was having a bad day. So was the guy who came in to relieve him.

In the top of the sixth the first batter poked an easy grounder to short and Heyman misplayed it, letting the ball roll through into left center, and Coach came off the bench like a skyrocket. "Rivers! Go in for Heyman! And for God's sake, no errors!"

Whoa! Mega stress! I grabbed my glove and ran out onto the field as Coach called Heyman in to the bench. The umps gave me a few warm ups and then play started again. The first thing I noticed was that my stomach was calm. In fact all of me was calm. I was thinking baseball, I was into it.

Usually, with a right-handed batter up and a guy on first,

the shortstop stays at home, letting the second baseman cover on the steal because the batter is more likely to hit a ball to the left side of the infield. Sometimes the batter counts on that, and tries to hit behind the runner, through the hole left by the second baseman when he goes to cover second. It's called a hit and run. But sometimes you get your pitcher to keep the ball low and outside so the batter has to hit it to second ... so that the shortstop can cover and maybe you get the double play. But not even the pros can do that all the time. The best I could hope for was to cheat a little toward second because Jake was kind of wild and usually he was wild to the outside edge of the plate. I took one step, and then after the batter swung and missed, I took another step because the guy was swinging late and there was no way he could it hit to the left side.

It worked perfectly. The batter swung and sent a fast grounder to Henry who picked it up, turned, and fired a perfect shot to me as I came across the bag and fired to first for the double play. Then we tossed it around the infield and got ready for the next batter.

He was their best hitter, as he'd proven all afternoon, but now Jake had gotten a shot of confidence and he challenged him up high. The guy bit and swung underneath the ball. Jake is a good pitcher, maybe the best on the team because he thinks. He threw his curve on the next pitch, keeping it to the outside of the plate and the guy let it go for a strike. But like all pitchers, Jake got cocky and challenged the guy again with his fastball and this time he put it over the plate belt high and the guy drove it toward the hole between short and third and I went for it, two steps and a rolling dive and I came up with the ball, set my feet and fired as hard as I could to first. I got him by half a step.

Our fans were going wild as we trotted in from the field and when I looked at Coach he smiled and nodded.

Henry clapped me on the shoulder. "Way to go, Nick!"

The manager called out the batting order. "Brodeur, Rivers, Dufresne!"

I pulled on my batting gloves, got two bats from my bag and stepped into the on-deck circle. You often hear sports announcers talk about a player being in the zone, and on that afternoon I was in the zone. It was like the light was brighter, the air especially clear.

Brodeur went down on four pitches, the way most of the guys had for five innings. Their pitcher was a big guy, six-five, maybe two hundred and twenty pounds, and he could throw really hard. The rumor was that he was signing with the Cubs as soon as he graduated. For sure, at almost five-eleven and one-sixty I didn't look like much of a threat, so maybe he didn't concentrate as hard.

His first pitch was off the plate inside, but I kept my feet planted and just leaned back a little to make sure I didn't get hit. The next pitch was closer and again I let it go past without moving my feet.

I wondered whether he was trying to throw at me like the guys do in the majors, but I didn't think he could be that good. Not that it mattered because the last thing he wanted to do now was throw another ball.

I decided to play with his head and just as he got ready to pitch I called for time and the ump shouted, "Time! No pitch!"

It broke the guy's rhythm and he kind of stumbled as he tried to hold up and then he threw the ball to the catcher, while I pretended to have something in my eye.

"Okay, batter?" the ump asked.

"Yup." I stepped in and waited and I got the pitch I wanted, a straight fastball just above the knees and I whipped my bat into it and sent a line drive right over the pitcher's head into center.

More cheering. It was like the days in Little League when I had been the star of the team.

Henry came up next and the pitcher had lost his groove and his head was out of the game. He walked Henry on four straight pitches and that's when his coach came out to the mound and called for a reliever.

Another tall guy, but this time a guy who threw sidearm and he scared the crap out of Tommy Johnson, who swung and missed three times out of self defense. Wilson Smart fared no better, his bat getting nothing but air.

The last inning was a non event. They didn't score and we didn't score and we had started the season zero and one.

Coach never said a word. He smiled at me once and that was all. Of course I was expecting him to tell me I was now the starting shortstop. But whether he said anything or not, I knew I'd made my mark. I hadn't just played, I'd played well and somewhere down the road that would add up.

But here's the thing that blew my doors off. I mean, if I put this in your tank it would start your engine. The zit was gone! Completely, absolutely, totally utterly gone! Not only had I measured up on the field, but I'd found a cure for zits! Naturally, I could see that it wasn't a cure for everyone, because you couldn't exactly put it in a bottle, advertise it on TV with a pretty girl who never had a zit in her life, and sell it by the truckload, but it had worked for me and as far as I was concerned, that meant it was a cure.

Here is what I have to say about the dance. I'm never going to another one. Here is why. I got to dance with Cindy just once all night. I spent a whole week fantasizing about how cool it would be dancing with her over and over and I got to dance with her just once because she had to hang out with the girls and then a lot of other, older guys danced with her, and I ended up with Paul and Ronnie which was not what I had planned.

Part of the problem was being a sophomore. The freshman girls are all giggly kids and the sophomore girls only want the juniors and seniors. Well, ask yourself this. When was the last time any older girl ever even allowed a sophomore boy to brush against her in the hall. I thought maybe it would be best to become a monk, but then I remembered the story I had once heard from Uncle Joe at a family party.

He had gone to a seminary to become a monk and the first summer he was there they had to shovel the coal out of this enormous coal bin, load it into wheelbarrows, and dump it down by the dock on the lake. It took them half the summer, and when they finished they were told to load the coal back into the wheelbarrows and dump it back into the coal bin. It was supposed to teach them discipline. Monkwork. It's my own word. I made it up to describe dumb jobs. Uncle Joe now makes a pile of money writing software.

Going to a dance is like wheeling loads of coal down to the lake and then being told to lug it back. You're letting someone else run your show and the only way you can beat them is to quit. At all costs you have to avoid monkwork. Of course, there is a small problem with that. School is monkwork, the worst kind of monkwork. Kids only go to school because there is no choice.

Once, when I was in sixth grade in our really stupid middle school where all the teachers and administrators are women and all the janitors are men, my parents talked about home schooling. They had some people in, and then some other people in and they even talked to my school principal, Mrs. Blunt. I remember her explanation particularly well, because it made no sense at all.

"One of the strongest reasons for Nicky to stay in the school," she said, "is the socialization skills he will learn. By himself everyday, he will become isolated from kids his own age and he will not develop properly."

It took me a while to figure that one out. You've probably noticed by now that I spend a lot of time thinking. I can't help it. Somebody says something like Mrs. Blunt did, and I immediately get the feeling that she is really saying something else and it bothers me until I understand what is really going on. What finally tipped me off was her claim that socialization was important. It isn't. It's dumb. Sports are important, even studies are important, but as far as I could see, my socialization skills were just fine. I had my buddies and I got along well with the guys on the baseball team, so what more did I need?

My mother agreed immediately and enthusiastically with Mrs. Blunt. Dad looked confused. I had no idea what had happened.

Here is what happened. Without saying it, Mrs. Blunt got a message across to Mom, which only a mom could understand. Boys need to be around so girls can practice *their* social skills on them. Girls are maximum into everything social, and boys are not. The reason they are not is because everything social is indirect and skirts the issue. It is vague and (here's a good word for the SATs) ambiguous. Boys like to pin things down. They like to know where they stand. Just like the dance? I thought I knew where I stood, but when I got there, I was totally in the dark.

I began to think that maybe I'd transfer to a private school for boys. Then all I'd have to worry about was gays and bullies and I figured I could handle those two categories pretty easily because I can run real fast and I'm nasty in a fight.

"That was fun," Ron said sarcastically as he climbed into the back seat and Paul climbed into the front.

"Sucked!" Paul said. "Absolutely sucked."

"I'm never going to another dance," I said. I started the car, turned on the lights, made sure everyone had their seat belt on, and then pulled out. "I need something to eat."

"Caruso's for pizza?" Ron asked.

"Sure," Paul said.

"Caruso's it is," I said.

"Did I hear right?" Paul asked. "Did I hear that you made two great plays and got a hit in the game this afternoon?"

I grinned. "Yeah. Heyman kept making errors so Coach put me in and hey, what can I tell you?" I waited for them to draw the wrong conclusion, expecting me to boast, then added, "I got lucky."

"What a piece of work," Ronnie said.

"You gonna start?" Paul asked.

"Coach didn't say anything at all. No compliment, not even a, 'hey, good play there, Nick.' Nothing at all."

"My brother says he's a weird guy like that. He never tells anyone they did something right, only that they did something wrong."

"I don't think I want to go to Caruso's," I said. "It'll be packed with kids from the dance."

"You got that right," Paul said.

"What about that new place that opened?" Ronnie asked.

"I heard it was like a country music joint," Paul said.

"Whoa, what's that all about ..." Ronnie said.

"On the other hand," I said. "Nobody from the dance will be in a country music joint, right?"

"I hear they serve really great pizza," Paul said.

"Let's give it a try."

It took awhile to get there, because it was on the far side of town. There wasn't much of a crowd, but the pizza smelled great and we sat at a table and the waitress came over with the menus.

"You want something to drink?" she asked.

We ordered sodas and then looked at the menu, finally deciding on three large pizzas with sausage and hamburg and extra cheese.

There were people at four other tables and the juke box was playing but it wasn't country music so much as folk music. It wasn't the stuff we listened to by a long shot, but it was okay, and I even found myself listening to it, and then a song came on about a guy who kills his girl because she won't marry him. I think it was called *The Banks of the Ohio* but I'm not sure. Anyway, those were the words in the refrain and I haven't got any idea why the song caught my attention, but it did. Maybe because the singer had this really nice clear voice that was pleasant and soothing.

And that put me in mind of something else. When I was younger I could remember Mom playing the guitar and singing. And there was always some joke about it, something about her hippie days. What struck me as odd was that I couldn't remember whether she had a nice voice or not.

"So," Paul said, " the wood bat worked, huh?"

"Yeah."

"I talked to at least five guys on your team at the dance and they're all going for wood bats." He grinned. "I think ballplayers are more superstitious than golfers."

"All jocks are superstitious," Ronnie said. "When I'm playing soccer, I never change my outside socks the whole season."

"Yeah, tell me about it," Paul said. "I sit next to you on the bus, remember?" He laughed. "It got so bad by the middle of November that Coach made us sit in the back of the bus with the windows open."

The waitress brought out the pizzas, big and juicy and hot and we dug in. For awhile, for three slices each, we said nothing. We simply pigged out.

"Hey," Ronnie said, "I don't care what kind of music they play here, this is the best pizza in town by far."

Both Paul and I agreed and kept on eating and pretty soon we had to order more pizzas because one each is never enough for three hungry guys who have just been to hell and back.

Then we were quiet for awhile because there is nothing social about pizza. It's there, it's good, you eat it, and you eat it until it's gone. Not only was the pizza good, but when they said large, they meant large, bigger by far than any other large pizza around.

Finally, when there was not a crust left, we sat back into our chairs and relaxed.

"You know," Ronnie said, "we ought to spread the word about this place."

"Just tell the guys," I said.

"Whoa," Paul laughed. "Is this guy pissed? I think this guy is pissed, I mean like totally, completely pissed. What the hell did she say to you, dude?"

"Nothing. I went there thinking I was gonna dance with her and she danced with all older guys. I danced with her once. What confuses me is that I thought I understood her when I talked to her on Monday, but it's pretty clear I had the wrong idea and I can't see how I could have gotten the wrong idea."

"Forget about it," Paul said. "Girls always do stuff like that."

"I thought it would help having an older sister, but all she ever did was boss me around," I said. "She even told me what clothes to wear."

We were generally agreed, in as much as we each had one, that older sisters sucked. In fact, the only things that didn't suck were the pizza we'd just eaten, baseball and golf and the fact that we were playing golf together tomorrow afternoon. We also agreed only to tell guys about the pizza here and tell them not to bring their dates. Not that we believed that would work, because once the girls knew the guys came here, the place would be full. Any place where guys gather, girls find out about ... fast!

On our way home we took a short cut over Rocky Road and I was just driving along, taking my time and we were talking about all kinds of stuff when I noticed a car up ahead that kept stopping and then starting up.

"Damn! Look at that," Paul said. "Somebody must've just smashed that mailbox." He pointed up ahead where a black mailbox, sat on its post, its door hanging open and its spine smashed flat so the ends stuck up at about forty-five degrees.

"There's another one!" Ronnie said.

"Look. There's the car!" I shouted. "Watch!"

The brake lights went on, the door flew open and a guy jumped out with a baseball bat and smashed the mailbox. Then he jumped back into the car and they headed down the road, skipping one and attacking the next. I let the car cruise closer. "Can you see who it is?"

"That's Hamm's car!" Paul said.

Suddenly we were right on them as the bat man leaped out of the car and was dumb enough to look back at us, right into the lights.

"That's Mike Oliver!"

KLANG! The bat came down into the spine of the mailbox and they took off.

"I'm outta here," I said, and at the crossroad I turned onto Center Road and headed back out to the main road.

"What's the big deal?" Ronnie asked. "They're just smashing mailboxes. I mean, it's like practically an Olympic sport around here."

"It's also a federal offense," I said.

"No way," Paul said.

"Yeah, it is," I said. "Ask your parents. And the guys that blow them up are looking at two federal offenses, one for destroying federal property and one for making a bomb."

"So what," Ronnie said. "No one ever gets caught."

"You wanna know what could happen here? I was the second car. Somebody hears the noise, they look out the window and they see my car. Maybe they get a license number. But even if they don't, I'm driving a white Volvo wagon and how many of those are there in town? Four? Five? So the cops talk to every owner and find out I was driving the car on Friday night at about the right time. Then they find out I play baseball which means I must own a baseball bat, and that's enough to make me guilty."

"Man, you do get out there in a hurry," Paul said.

"Com'on, Nick, get real," Ronnie said. "Nobody's quick enough to get to the window that fast."

"Right, but this is also the time of night when people walk their dogs."

"It's no big deal, Nick," Paul said. "You got two witnesses and we identified the guys who were doing it."

"And you're gonna turn in Mike Oliver, right?"

That quieted them down, because if there was one really mean and nasty guy in the whole high school it was Mike Oliver. The guy had muscles that science hadn't named yet.

EIGHT

The First Visit

On Saturday I got up late, ten-thirty to be exact, showered, and went downstairs, knowing that I'd have to scrounge up my own breakfast. Don't you hate having to do stuff like that? I never know what I want to eat. All I know is I'm hungry. Scrounging for lunch is okay because there's always some kind of meat around, but breakfast? Hey, no bagels, no breakfast.

There was a note stuck to the refrigerator door saying that Dad was playing golf and Mom and Lizzie had gone to the mall (where else?).

The next thing I did was check the garage to make sure somebody had left me a car, and I was some relieved when I opened the door and Dad's Honda Civic was sitting there. In another month both Paul and Ronnie would have their licenses, but for now I was the only one of us who could drive.

Hunger rules. I got some cereal and slid into the breakfast nook which had windows on three sides. The sun was out again and it already looked warm. Perfect for the batting cages. I still had a couple of hours to kill and I was thinking I'd plug into some Nintendo, when I looked up and there, on the hill, was Mr. Bede, bending over a pile of junk, pulling pieces out and discarding them until he found one he liked. He stood, scarecrow lean, silhouetted against the morning sky, examining his treasure and then he turned and walked back toward the house.

Suddenly I knew what I was going to do for the next couple of hours, and to make sure I didn't back out, I finished my cereal and left the house immediately, walking with absolute determination up the hill. It seemed steeper than I remembered and the higher I climbed, the harder I worked. Each step felt as if I were walking in heavy mud that sucked at my shoes. I felt like a battery-powered toy whose power was fading fast. Finally, almost at the top, and just when I could see past the bushes and trees alongside the road to his house, I stopped, unable to move even a single step closer.

So there I stood, by the road, trying not to look conspicuous, which is impossible when you stop alongside a country road, because there are no other humans around, and nothing is more conspicuous than a human standing alone.

The voice, alive with irony and humor startled me so badly that I inhaled sharply and nearly lost my jeans.

"Well, you got that far, a couple more steps ought to get it done, don't you think?"

There was Augustus Bede IV, standing by a junkpile, grinning at me from one of the most pleasant faces I'd ever seen.

I suppose I've looked foolish now and then, but I certainly never felt any more foolish.

"Of course, I can see you've been somewhat struck by my reputation, so I guess that explains your silence."

Lie, I said to myself, lie like mad, but I couldn't think of anything to lie about. "I meant to bring my new bats," I said.

He looked puzzled but only for a second. "The ones Tom makes. He told you about the machine I built for him, then."

"Yes, sir," I said. My feet had begun to feel a good deal lighter. "I never met an inventor before."

He smiled warmly. "Well, you have now. I'm Augustus Bede, which I suspect you already know, and if I'm guessing right you're Nick Rivers. First house down the hill."

I nodded, stunned that he knew who I was, and feeling very uneasy because it's no good having adults know who you are.

"I'm in your debt," he said. "If you hadn't gone asking questions, you wouldn't have gotten an old friend stirred up enough to pay a call." He grinned at me. "Com'on ashore," he said. "I like a curious mind."

And with that I did it. I stepped onto his property and walked over to where he was standing. But I had no idea what to say and he seemed to understand that.

"Would you care to see what an inventor invents?"

"Yes, I would."

"Come along then and have a look." He stopped and scanned his yard and the piles of junk. "I suppose to most folks this looks like a scrap yard, but to me it's Aladdin's treasure cave." He pointed to the pile he'd been digging through. "This pile is all round bar stock. That one is angle

iron. That one is flat stock. I keep saying that one day I'll
store it all in the barn where it won't rust, but the rust causes
no problem for my purposes and I just can't see wasting the
time. I'd rather spend my time on something useful. Some
might say I'd save time in the end because I wouldn't have
to look through the pile. But the way I see it, that's kind of
like using the dictionary on the computer where you only
see a few words at a time. With a real dictionary you always
light on something unexpected as you turn the pages looking for the word you want. I go rooting through a pile and
suddenly I see something I hadn't seen before and that starts
me thinking and before you know it I'm inside drafting up a
new device."

"I think it bothers the women mostly," I said.

He grinned. "They do prefer neat yards, as a rule."

He turned toward the house and I walked alongside. I
hadn't stood beside many men that tall before, but he seemed
even taller because he was so thin.

"And I'd guess that it doesn't bother your dad as much?"

"He's an engineer," I said.

"What kind?"

"Mechanical."

"You'll have to bring him by sometime."

"He'd like that."

"No need to stand on ceremony. Just stop by."

He held the door and I stepped into the house, aware
that I wasn't one tiny bit worried. I'd have bet my life on the
fact that Mr. Bede was the least dangerous man in the world.

The front entry hall had doors to either side, one of which
was open and this was the very room I had been looking into

with my telescope. It gave me kind of an eerie feeling as I followed him into the large room, almost as if someone were watching me from my room at home.

"This used to be a living room," he said, "but I needed a shop in the house where it was convenient and a lot warmer. You get to my age and the blood doesn't circulate as well."

Work benches and machines lined the walls between the four windows and a fireplace on the inside wall. A large drawing table with a stool squatted in the center of the room next to a long table also equipped with comfortable stools.

"I chose this room because it faces south and west and in the winter I like as much sunlight as I can get." He pointed up to the banks of high power lighting which ran in rows across the ceiling. "I also like it as bright as I can get it. Old eyes need plenty of light."

I had no idea what I was looking at. I mean, I knew they were machines but I had no idea what kind of machines or what they were used for, except one. The lathe. I knew about that from Mr. Baines' shop. "What kind of things are you working on?" I asked.

"Well, a lot of it is pretty secret stuff. Not government stuff," he added quickly. "Industrial. That's mostly what I do now. A company comes to me with a problem they haven't been able to solve and I find a solution."

"The way you did for Mr. Baines."

"Exactly the same. That was quite a nifty little machine. The trick was how to harden the wood to a uniform density, which was complicated because a bat is not only round, but tapers in diameter. In the end I fashioned a laser reader to the machine to control the position of the rollers. But that still would have left flat spots so I devised a little computer program which increases the hydraulic pressure minutely each time the bat goes through the rollers. It also rotates the bat every so slightly each time. But the key is the number of passes each bat makes. With enough passes the flat spots are eliminated."

"How many times does each bat go through?"

"I found that a hundred and twenty-one passes took care of the problem. But of course, that had to happen rapidly, otherwise it so lengthened the time of completion that it was impractical even for a small operation like Tom's. Each bat takes twenty seconds." He grinned. "It's a lot to happen in twenty seconds. Just the sort of problem I like to work out."

"I saw the machine work," I said. "But it's covered so all I saw was the bat go in and the bat come out. I had no idea all that was going on."

"Do you play computer games?" he asked.

"Sure. Every kid does."

"Then I guess I'm still a kid. I love the darn things. I'm even writing a couple of my own." He sat on one of the stools. "Of course they're kind of educational, but maybe no one will notice that too much."

"Educational games are pretty noticeable," I said.

"Well, maybe not this one. It's designed for the new Nintendo and not a computer as such, and it's a search for treasure but it all takes place inside an automobile engine."

I thought that sounded pretty cool. "Is it ready to be played?"

"Not yet. When I'm ready, you can be my test pilot."

"Wow, really?"

"Sure. Everything has to be tested, you know." He looked at me and smiled. "Have you tested out your new bat?"

"Yup."

"How did it work?"

"Amazing. Totally amazing. I got into the game on Friday and I actually got a hit. Now a whole bunch of the guys want to buy Mr. Baines' bats."

"As well they should. Those bats are really special. You can't imagine the trouble he goes to just to get the right wood. He's got over fifty sawmills pulling wood and setting it aside just for him. Did he show you the flex tester?"

"I'm not sure. He showed us a lot of stuff all at once."

"That machine he built himself. Even got a patent for it. He built it to hold the bat and swing it through a light field at a given speed. The light field is equipped with strobe lights that allow him to video tape the bat and measure the degree of flex. By doing that he found which grain configuration in the wood produced the amount of flex he wanted."

Don't ask me why, but I found all this talk very exciting. It was like stepping through a time warp or something. One second I knew nothing and then a couple of minutes later I knew things I had never imagined. And the more I knew, the more I wanted to know. This was an entirely new feeling. Mr. Bede showed me some of the projects he was working on and some of them were way beyond me. Even with his careful, very clear explanations I couldn't get a handle on them.

And then suddenly I realized I'd been there two hours and it was time to go, simply because I was worn out from trying to stuff so much into my brain all at once.

Of course, what I really wanted to ask him, I simply

couldn't ask. If he wanted to talk about what had happened to his wife, he would have to start the conversation and I was certain that he would not. Any information I discovered would have to come from other sources. But this much I knew. I liked Mr. Bede as well as anyone I had ever met and I was going to do everything I could to prove that he had not killed his wife. He just didn't deserve to have to live under such a cloud. In fact, what he deserved, was for everyone who lived in our town to understand and appreciate this incredible man.

And then he took me by surprise yet again.

"Wilson Jones told me that you were asking about me, and he told me why. I just want you to know that I have no objections to your questions, but I must admit to a certain curiosity."

"What some people say and what the newspaper stories say are different."

"You looked them up?"

"Over at UConn."

"A surprising young man, you are, Nick Rivers. Most surprising. Even enterprising. But what got you started?"

"I'm not really sure, or maybe I've forgotten, but it seems to me it was just a feeling, and then when I asked people it was pretty clear they only had rumors and guesses. It didn't seem fair."

He smiled. "In all the time that's passed since that horrible night, you are the only one who ever thought to ask. Would you like me to tell you what I know?"

"I don't want to upset you," I said.

"I appreciate that, Nick. And it still does, of course, but it was a long, long time ago and I've learned to live with it, as one must. The truth is, I don't know much. I had taken the boys down to Doctor Gray's for their annual checkup, as Mary had a cold. The appointment was late and it was dark by the time we returned. I called out and when she didn't answer I thought she must be asleep so I sent the boys upstairs and walked to the front of the house to turn on some lights. I found her in the parlor." He took a deep breath. "I checked her pulse, then I went out of the room, closed the door, called the police, and went upstairs to the boys. No one should ever have to go through such a thing."

My throat seemed as if it were swollen shut.

"It turned out that had I arrived home a minute or two sooner I would probably have caught the killer in the act. If the town hadn't put in the stop sign at the end of the road, I might have gotten here in time.

"The next day the police arrested me and charged me with murder and my aunt Margaret took the boys to her house. I wasn't in jail long, a week, only. The only reason they arrested me was that they couldn't think who else to arrest. Whoever killed her left no fingerprints or footprints. Nothing was stolen, there were no signs of a struggle. It must have either been someone she knew, or someone who took her completely by surprise. Perhaps both."

"I'll stop asking about it, if you want me to," I said.

"My only worry is that you may well discover something, and in the process frighten the murderer into coming after you. I'm sure you know the old adage about sleeping dogs."

I grinned. "But if you don't wake them up, you may never know what was under them."

He laughed. "You know, I am going to very much enjoy

having you as a neighbor, Nick. I like the way you think, and I like your courage." His voice changed, the tone implying the seriousness of what he had to say. "But remember this, Nick. Watch your back. This may well be dangerous."

"Yes, sir," I said.

"And drop by whenever you have the time."

"Thanks," I said.

When I got home the first thing I did was take a leak. I'd been holding it a long time because, well, who wants to ask somebody if you can use their bathroom? The second thing I did was call Ronnie and ask him whether he thought his mother could tell me who had known Mary Bede.

"You'll have to ask her," he said. "I'm not getting into that with her. She goes totally wild."

So I drove over to Ronnie's and found Mrs. Lathrop fixing lunch. I dove right in.

"Mrs. Lathrop," I asked. "Do you know anyone who knew Mrs. Bede?"

"What's this all about?" She looked up from the bacon frying slowly in the skillet.

"I spent two hours with Mr. Bede this morning and it's hard to believe that he could've, I mean, I just don't think he could've done it."

"And you're going to prove that he didn't?"

I shrugged. "Well, that's what I have in mind."

Now she stared at me ... hard and I could see she was angry, but that she was also trying to control it. "How could you prove it after so much time?"

"I don't know. Maybe I can't. I just want to find out as much as I can."

"What happens if you discover that he did it?"

"I hadn't thought of that."

"It's worth considering, don't you think?"

"I guess I'll have to consider that when I get there."

"But you don't think that's what you will find."

"No, I don't. I mean, how well do you know him?"

"I never knew him at all. I'm too young. But my cousin Rachel Mason was in the same class with Mary. They were close friends. She never understood why Mary married Augustus Bede. I don't think anyone did. She was such a beautiful girl and he is so homely and quiet. She was vivacious and had a million friends. Everybody liked Mary."

"Would she talk to me about Mary, do you think?"

"Why are you so interested in Mary? Wouldn't it be better to learn more about Augustus?"

"I'm doing both. I already talked to Paul's grandfather. It was pretty interesting. But I figured that it was Mary who was murdered, and if Mr. Bede didn't kill her then maybe there was something in Mary's past that led to the killing. I'm sure the police looked into that, but then maybe they didn't ask the right questions. Maybe they never asked any questions at all, because they arrested Mr. Bede real fast and then after the case was thrown out they quit looking, at least according to the stories I read at the UConn library."

Adults, as a rule do not take teenagers seriously, so you have to gather your information and your ideas carefully and then go in with your guns blazing. Always mention libraries. Adults have a high opinion of kids who go to libraries.

"I mean suppose there was something that happened that hardly anyone knew about, maybe something that at the time seemed so small that nobody gave it a second thought?"

She had completely forgotten about the bacon, and for the first time I began to think maybe I had introduced some doubt.

"Rachel has always said he must have done it, so I'm not sure she would even agree to talk to you. But just now you said something that made me think. Every time I read in the newspapers about some celebrated murder case where the police acted very quickly, the accused gets acquitted. Augustus was arrested within twenty-four hours." She flipped the bacon. "I'll ask Rachel and I'll have Ronnie call and take you over there. She likes Ronnie."

"Thanks, Mrs. Lathrop, I really appreciate your help."

Suddenly a frown appeared on her face. "But you'd better be careful here, Nick. If you're right, then there's a murderer out there and he might not be very happy about someone digging into this."

It sent a shiver up my spine. That was two people who had thought of the same thing and it was getting clearer that I could get in over my head real fast. But hey, in for a penny, in for a pound, as Dad always says. "I'd still like to talk to your cousin."

"I'll arrange it then. And you'll stay to lunch, won't you?" She grinned, having caught me staring at the bacon. Nobody can be in a kitchen with bacon frying and not start drooling, not even my friend Ben, who is Jewish and doesn't eat pork. One time he was at the house for lunch and Mom forgot and was making BLT's. I had to remind her and Ben got mystery meat. Talk about getting a sandwich at a banquet!

"I was hoping you'd ask," I said. "Thanks."

NINE

A Visit With Rachel

Cousin Rachel looked a lot older than Mr. Bede, though she was younger by ten years. She had pure white hair and she was kind of round the way most grandmothers are round and she had a warm smile and pale blue eyes hidden by her gold rimmed glasses. Ronnie had told me she suffered from arthritis and that she couldn't walk very well and her hands were badly crippled, but that she still always had a batch of sugar cookies ready whenever he came to visit.

And as it turned out she had some on hand that Sunday and plenty of cold milk to go with them and what's more she wanted to talk about Mary.

"Oh, we were the best of friends," she said. "We did everything together all the way through high school. Then I went to college to become a teacher, and Mary, who was ever so much smarter than any of the rest of us, went to Radcliffe. We all expected she would become a doctor or a movie star, which was why we were so surprised when she took up with Augustus. I've thought a good deal about that over the years and I think maybe we were a little resentful. I guess I thought Mary was going to put our little town on the map. She was so brilliant and so beautiful and so very, very nice to everyone. But Augustus, well it wasn't that he wasn't nice, because he never, that I heard, ever turned down a request for help from anyone, even people he didn't much care for. It was just that, well, to tell the truth, he was not much favored by the girls. He was too brainy for one thing and he was so tall and skinny and his face was too long and he never talked much. In those days people didn't leave the way they do now. They went off to school or into the service but they almost always came back." She picked up the cup of tea Ronnie had made for her and, holding it between the gnarled fingers of both hands, sipped at the edge like a bird, gently and delicately.

"What did you want to know about Mary?"

"Who she liked or didn't like, who didn't like her."

"Everybody liked her. Especially the boys. I think they were all in love with her and that should have made the girls all hate her, but you couldn't hate Mary. And, after all, it wasn't her fault, and she surely never made any great thing about it. And she never dated a boy more than once or twice.

"Some of the boys made absolute fools of themselves, you know, showing off the way boys do ..." She looked up. "Do they still do that?"

I nodded and smiled, admitting that yes, in fact, we did, however much we hated ourselves afterward. "I just wish the girls were a little nicer, sometimes," I said.

"Are they so mean, really?"

"They sure are," Ronnie said. "Especially the girls our age. All they want is to date the juniors and seniors."

Rachel laughed. "And next year those girls who are freshmen now will want to date you because you're juniors. Pay it no mind. It all changes very quickly. Girls always like older boys, well most of them do, anyway. And certainly Mary did. Why Augustus was ten years older. Oh, the stories we heard. Some said he was robbing the cradle. Others said it was almost immoral because he was so much older. We were mean and petty, to be sure. But the truth, as is usually the case, was different. Augustus may have been ten years older, but he looked like a boy, and his enthusiasm was boundless. I haven't seen him in a long time," she said. "I've often wondered how he's aged."

"He still looks fifteen years younger than he is," I said. "And he works all the time. He's so busy that most of the time he seems to run rather than walk."

"Yes, I would have expected that. He's one of those men who'll live to be a hundred, busy, till one day he just dies."

I tried to think of a question that would allow her to go beyond what she had said, because I suspected that she, like my grandparents, had reduced some of her memories to passwords or labels. I remembered what had happened at the dance on Friday night and that helped. "Some of the boys must not have liked being dropped after a couple of dates," I said. "Maybe some were jealous of others."

"Why there were even fights," Rachel said. "I remember Billy Pearson and Hank Gray got into a terrible fight right outside of school one day and it took four men, two of them coaches, to break it up. Oh my, that was a terrible fight. And they were nice boys too. Neither of them had ever been in trouble before. All I ever knew was that the fight had something to do with Mary. My goodness, I'd quite forgotten that. They were both badly banged up. It was simply terrible. And they both got thrown out of school. The strangest thing was that they had always been close friends." She stopped for more tea. "Of course she didn't date every boy in the school, not even all the boys in her own class. She was very tall, you see, very tall, five foot seven if she was an inch. So she didn't date the shorter boys."

"Do any of the boys she dated still live in town?"

"Most of them, except for the ones who have died."

"Who's still here?" I asked.

"You know, I just got a list the other day in the alumni news letter. Ronnie, I think it's still on my desk, could you bring it over? And bring the pad and pencil next to it."

He got up quickly, fetched the items from the desk, and handed them to her.

"How are your cookies holding out?" she asked. "Humm, plates are empty I see. Why don't you both go get a refill and I'll go through the list."

By the time we came back from the kitchen she had nearly finished. I felt badly about that, because of her hands and how it must have hurt to write.

"Eight names," she said. "I would've thought there were more. But that's all I can be sure of. Of course it wasn't a very big school then, only forty-six of us, but I would have thought there were more living here." She tore the paper from the pad and I got up, took it, and sat back down.

"Now you read me the names and I'll tell you about them."
Her writing was amazingly clear and even, despite her
hands. "John Maynard," I read.

"Went to work at one of the mills. Married a girl from
Unity Falls. When his parents died he quit the mill, took
over the farm, and raised dairy cows. Did quite well. He
took Mary to the junior prom."

"Walter Windale."

"Walter went out with her once or twice. Took her to a
school dance. Nice boy. Went into the insurance business
with his father. Hard worker. He was in the Marines."

We went through the list, but nothing got my attention.

"I can see from the look on your face, that you didn't find
what you were looking for," she said.

"Well, I don't know, really. Maybe I have to think about
it. Or maybe I don't know enough about them. Like George
Paschendale. You didn't have much to say about him."

"I suppose I didn't." She made a face as if she'd just
bitten into a lemon. "I never liked him. He was sullen and
he always wore dirty clothes. The family was poor. The father was a drunkard, you see, and he couldn't hold a job.
Terrible family. He had an older brother, Arthur, who is even
stranger. Now, that's an interesting story. Arthur fought in
the Pacific and lost a leg. He came home and he had a full
pension so he didn't have to work and he built himself a
cabin on the family property and despite his injury got a job
in the mill as a weaver.

"He was a senior when we were freshmen and he always
used to scare us because he looked so mean. He had little
eyes and a big round face and he was very tall, almost as tall

as Augustus. He never would say a word, he'd just stare at us. All the girls were scared of him. I suppose it was pretty mean of us, because he couldn't help the way he looked, but I have to say there was something about him, when all is said and done. When the mill closed he started a business as a handyman, you know, doing odd jobs for people. He was very good at it, or so I've heard. Never married. And he's still living in his cabin and doing odd jobs, though not so much anymore because with his disability and his age, you know, it's not so easy to get things done."

"But you know, I never heard anyone say a harsh word against him. In fact when he came home they even had a parade and he rode in the front car with the head of the American Legion. Not only had he lost a leg, but he'd been awarded several medals for bravery. As far as I know he's never missed a Memorial Day parade since. He's always up there on the reviewing stand, just sitting and watching. A perfectly harmless man, by all accounts. But his brother George, well he's a different matter. He's been in prison at least three times. All three times for assault. Once he used a tire iron on another man. He was just lucky he didn't kill him." She sat still for a second, looking as if she had remembered something and either she decided not to say anything or she thought it wasn't important.

"Is he in prison now?" Ronnie asked.

"No. He lives with his wife and her parents in the old farmhouse and he has quite a nice orchard now."

"G.P.'s Orchard?" I asked.

"The very same," Rachel said.

"Everybody goes there," Ronnie said. "There's a very

nice lady who sells the apples and the honey."

"That's George's wife, Liz. And you're right, she is a very nice person. How she could have stayed married to George, no one knows. But in fairness to George, he didn't pick any of the fights he was in. He was set upon each time and he only went to jail because he responded so viciously."

She shifted around in the chair but the arthritis made it impossible to get comfortable. Clearly she was in pain, yet somehow she seemed to rise above it, and I wondered if I could do that. I didn't think so. I'm really a baby about pain, though I hate to admit it. Who would?

"Most of George's troubles came from being in bars and when he stopped going to bars, his troubles seemed to end. They have two children, both grown and moved away, and I hear he takes good care of his parents, who are both close to a hundred now. Of course, everybody expects he'll blow up again one day. A man like that, with a nasty temper, well, it's just a matter of time before something sets him off. Of course, the older he gets, the less likely it is that'll he'll get into a fight, I think. He's two years younger than his brother."

"I've never seen him at the apple store," I said.

"He never goes into the store. Everybody knows about his past, and he's afraid it will affect his business. And anyway, Liz takes care of that end of things."

It seemed as if I'd reached a dead end.

"Why are you interested in Mary?" she asked me.

"Mr. Bede lives just up the road from us and I've gotten to know him a little, and I just can't believe that anyone believes he could have killed someone."

"All humans have sides to them that we seldom ever see,"

she said. "Look at George Paschendale. If you didn't know about his past, you'd meet him and he would seem perhaps a bit odd, but you wouldn't suspect he was a violent man. And just suppose, for example, that Mary had taken up with another man. Suppose Augustus found himself facing a future without the only woman he had ever loved? How would that affect him? We can never know such things about people."

"Do you think he killed her?" I asked.

She smiled. "Are you always so blunt?"

"He drives the teachers crazy," Ronnie said.

"Nothing wrong with getting to the meat of things."

She hadn't answered my question and I couldn't ask it a second time. If she had wanted to answer, she would have. On the other hand I needed an answer. "Ronnie's mom thinks he did," I said.

"Do you have it in mind to prove that he didn't kill her?" Rachel asked.

"Yes, ma'am."

"Why would you stir it up after all these years?"

"At first I was just curious. Then I went over to UConn and read all the articles that were in the papers and the more I read, the more I thought that they were right to drop the charges. I know how I feel when I'm accused of doing something that I didn't do, and I began to wonder, if he didn't do it, then who did? In all the newspaper articles there wasn't anything about the police looking for another killer. I didn't even know Mr. Bede when I went over to UConn. All I knew were the stories about him. But after yesterday, after getting to know him a little, I just can't believe he's guilty, and yet a lot of people in town still think he's a murderer." I knew she was thinking that I ought to mind my own business because no sixteen-year-old was gonna solve anything, and all I'd do was stir up trouble. "Why do people think he did it?" I asked.

"You asked me whether I thought he killed poor Mary and I didn't answer. I didn't because something in me always led me to think he must have done it. Now, I wonder why I never asked myself who else might have?" She pulled herself up in the chair and her eyes were alive with light. "Augustus Bede is a genius and even though people value such genius, they fear it at the same time. We are brought up to believe that such people are odd and unpredictable. We are told that they are different, even unstable. When you talk to someone who has such an enormous I.Q., you always feel as though they are not quite there. You resent the fact that they know things you cannot possibly understand, and out of that comes fear and finally dislike and mistrust. As a teacher I had to fight that all my life. Year after year I always found one or two students in my classes who were very bright, far brighter than I am, and they always made me nervous. It was almost as if they spoke a different language. It took all I had to find things to keep them busy, and I was never truly successful at it. They devoured the most complicated ideas and concepts effortlessly. But not one of them could hold a candle to Augustus Bede. He went through the best colleges and universities as if they were child's play." She looked off toward the window, silent and still.

Neither Ronnie nor I said anything. It was as if she were frozen in time like a painting.

And finally she spoke. "I think I have done Augustus Bede a grave injustice. In fact this entire town has done him a massive injustice. We offered no help. Even those who thought he was innocent did not come forward. We left him alone with two boys to raise and no one offered a hand. And he did a fine job with his sons. He educated them at home and they are both highly successful men with good families, from what I hear. I suppose we could justify our behavior by saying that a man like Augustus Bede prefers to be alone, that he is so busy that other human company doesn't matter to him. But I don't think that can be true. All of us, at some point in every day, need to talk to someone even if it is no more than some little conversation about the weather or what's for dinner. My husband and I treasure those moments. And Augustus has none." She smiled. "How he must have enjoyed your visit," she said.

"I don't think he could have enjoyed it more than I did. I never learned so much in such a short time, and this was interesting stuff, useful stuff."

"I owe you a debt of gratitude, Nick. If you hadn't come here today I might have gone to my grave never once having had a kind thought for Augustus. I might never have said a thing about him to anyone else. And that is no way for someone who thinks of herself as a Christian to have behaved."

It was the second time I'd heard that and it was beginning to make me uneasy. Just what *had* I gotten myself into? And if people began to talk, what might suddenly turn up that I couldn't anticipate? The only solace I could find was in knowing that at least two people now thought differently about Mr. Bede. Perhaps, I thought, even if I never find out who killed Mary Bede, it won't matter because just asking questions was changing things.

I'll tell you this. My head was spinning and my brain was sorely overworked. I needed to play ball. I needed to break a sweat, and even though I was a rotten golfer I was looking forward to playing golf with Paul and Ronnie.

I stood up. "Thank you very much for talking with me."

She smiled and pulled herself from the chair, balancing with her canes. "This has been a most stimulating discussion. Just wait till Roger gets in from cutting the grass. I'll probably chew his ear off."

She walked with us to the door, using her canes and shuffling her feet.

"And thanks for the cookies and milk too," I said. "Those are the best sugar cookies I've ever eaten."

Ronnie grinned. "I told you."

☞   ☞   ☞

"Well," Ronnie asked as I started the car, "did you find out what you wanted?"

"I don't know."

"Do you know what you're looking for?"

"Good question." I backed out of the driveway, looking both ways at the road, and then headed off toward Paul's. "She made a lot of sense," I said. "Especially about not knowing much about other people. I hadn't thought of that."

"This could really stir up a lot of trouble. Rachel's right about that too. Just look at my mom. She gets all worked up about it."

"But she did talk to Rachel for me."

"I gotta admit that took me by surprise."

"What do you think? Did he do it?"

"I don't think anything about this. I don't even want to think about this. Dad says I have to get a B in geometry and that's what I'm spending my time thinking about."

"Why didn't you ask me for help?"

"I don't know."

"From now on we'll do our homework together, okay?"

"Will it get me a B?"

"How hard do you want to work?"

"I hate geometry."

"That just means you'll have to work harder."

"I didn't hate algebra," Ronnie said. He groaned. "All I want to do is play golf. I'm thinking maybe a couple of years of college and then I'll go to qualifying school."

"Don't give up your day job," I said.

"What's that supposed to mean?"

"Study the geometry. You'll need it for the SATs."

"You sound like a teacher, Nick, and it's not good to sound like a teacher when you're still a kid. It confuses people."

I laughed. Suddenly I felt good, the way you do when things are going just right, but I couldn't think what had brought that on, especially since I was going to play golf and I am a lousy golfer. "I'll make you a deal. I'll get you straight with geometry if you'll get my golf swing straightened out."

"Hey, that's easy, dude. I told you a thousand times already. Don't swing so hard. You keep trying to kill the ball."

"I swing too hard at everything," I said.

TEN

Truth To Tell

"I hate school." I toyed with my Sugar Frosted Flakes.

"It's your job," Dad said, without looking up from his Corn Flakes.

"But when you don't like a job, you quit," I said.

"And what do you do after you quit? Do you think another employer wants to hire you?"

I also hate questions like that because there's only one answer.

"I like school," Lizzie said.

I scowled around at her, but she wasn't about to back down. She had a good thing going and she knew it. Cute little girls can get anything they want just by buttering everybody up, and Lizzie is an expert, having watched her older sister. In a situation like that, go for damage control; change the subject. I remembered I hadn't said anything about the game on Friday and I launched into it.

"I got into the game on Friday and I got a hit and I made two great plays at shortstop and ..."

Dad looked up from his Corn Flakes. "You didn't tell me that." He frowned. "And I thought you played second."

"Now I think maybe I'm a shortstop."

"I can't believe you never told us," Mom said.

"That's because this is the first time we've all been at the same table since breakfast on Friday."

"It is not!" Mom said.

"Yes it is," Lizzie said.

I could have kissed her ... if she weren't my sister.

"I can't believe we did that," Mom said. Then she looked at me. "But I can understand how it happened. You've just got too many irons in the fire, Nick."

"Hey, I was here for breakfast and dinner on Saturday and for all three meals on Sunday. I didn't even know where the rest of you went except to the mall and golfing. Nobody even left a note after the ones on Saturday."

"When's your next game?" Dad asked. See? Damage control; change the subject.

"Tomorrow at Thurston."

"What time?"

"Three."

"I'll be there," he said.

"I probably won't play."

"Why not? I thought you said ..."

"Maybe I'll find out at practice today. But Coach never said anything, and I made two really great plays. One of them was a double play."

"I take it the new bat worked?"

"I never hit a ball better in my life. It was a smokin' line drive right over the pitcher into center. I got all of it."

Mom was still in shock about the weekend meals. "I can't believe we didn't eat together," she said. "I feel just awful!"

"I also had a nice talk with Mr. Bede Saturday morning. He showed me around his shop and showed me what he's working on. I never saw so much interesting stuff."

That got Mom's attention. "You went up there? You talked to him?" She looked like I'd surrendered to the anti-Christ. "Do you have any idea how dangerous he is! You could have been ... murdered!"

"Mom, he's not what you think."

"Oh yes he is!"

"How do you know?"

"I just know. People who don't wave and leave trash in their yards are not to be trusted. And what's more I think it's pretty clear that he killed his wife."

I looked to Dad for help, but he shrugged and looked down at his Corn Flakes. Every morning he eats Corn Flakes and he doesn't even put sugar on them. Adults are strange.

"Mom and I had dinner at Wendy's," Lizzie said. "Two nights in a row!"

"The malls were absolutely jammed," Mom said. She looked accusingly at Dad. "And where did you get off to?"

"Saturday afternoon I played golf with Will Tennerson and I called but I got no answer, so I had dinner at the club. Sunday I was down at Tom Baines' shop and I just forgot what time it was. By the time I got home you were all here so I assumed you'd just eaten without me, and I fixed up some leftovers and got indigestion watching '60 Minutes'."

"This is awful! Do you realize what's happening here? We are becoming a dysfunctional family, for Pete's sake."

Now that was something I didn't want to hear. Not that we were becoming dysfunctional, because we weren't. The trouble was that now Mom thought we were, and that would mean all sorts of family togetherness stuff. I'm not saying I don't like my family, because I like them all a lot, even Beth. It's just that when Mom gets off on a cause like that everybody loses the freedom to do what they want.

"Look, it's okay, Mom, really. I spent a lot of time studying and I got way ahead for the week. And right now, with baseball, and Ronnie and Paul trying to straighten out my golf game, I need all the time I can get for studying." More lies. Well, not real lies, I mean the kind where you gain at someone else's expense, but the kind where you are just trying to protect yourself. And anyway, lying is an art form. So is the truth. "After you worked with me on studying for biology I started doing it in all my courses. It takes a lot of time, but, I gotta tell you, Mom, it really pays off. You oughta start with Lizzie right now so by the time she gets to high school it'll be like second nature. I can't believe how much better I did."

Did that please her? Of course. Was it the truth? Well ... as a matter of fact, it was the absolute unvarnished truth. I had used her system and I had done a lot better. In fact, I did so much better that I was looking forward to getting my work done. Of course, you never admit stuff like that to your parents. It raises the level of what they expect.

Then I tried a new tack. "Say, Dad, I've been thinking how it would be a lot more convenient for everyone if I had my own car. Nothing fancy, just good solid transportation. Something safe, like an old Volvo. I could even learn how to fix stuff when it breaks. But most of all neither of you would have to waste your time lugging me all over the place."

Dead silence. No outrage. No nothing, and I wondered if maybe Dad had gotten a raise.

"How much can you pay toward a car?" he asked.

"I've got three thousand saved up."

"Really? And you'd spend it on a car?"

"Sure. But after that I'll be tapped out, and with base-ball, there's no way I can work, and anyway, I don't want to work. It'll cut into the time I spend on my studies."

Oh, I am good! I am the best! With political skills like that I could run for President.

Dad finished his Corn Flakes, even the soggy ones at the bottom. It made me sick. "Let's talk some more about this at dinner, after your mother and I have had a chance to talk."

And I left it there. Not that I didn't have more to say, because I always have more to say, but there are times when things are better left unsaid.

☞   ☞   ☞

At the end of the day, just before baseball practice I was summoned to the office where the Toad awaited. Only this time she had help. We met in the principal's office along with the principal, Mr. Allen, the assistant principal, Mr. Kearns, the Toad, and a state cop, Trooper Gazerelli.

"Sit down, Nick," Mr. Allen said.

It was the first time I had ever seen him close up, and I

sat in the only empty chair and waited. It is hard to believe that you can be alone in a room full of people, but as a student, a kid, surrounded by every authority figure they could scrape up, I felt absolutely alone.

"We have a report that you were seen smashing mailboxes on Friday night." The Toad stared, eyes unblinking.

"I didn't smash any mailboxes."

"We have an eyewitness," she said.

I guess I'm not really very smart. I mean, I could've played dumb, but I get pissed off when I've been accused of something I didn't do. And when I'm mad I tend to attack. Everybody always says the best offense is a good defense but when someone attacks, I counter attack! On the other hand, you don't go crazy. Argue. My mother thinks I'm gonna wind up as a lawyer, but I'm thinking Red Sox.

"You can't have an eyewitness, because I didn't smash any mailboxes."

"You're saying this person is lying?" Mr. Allen asked.

"No, sir. I'm only saying they didn't see what they thought they saw. I mean, they probably believe they saw what happened, but in reality they didn't."

I could feel the trooper's eyes boring into me, but he said nothing. The Toad, however was building up a full head of steam. She was practically levitating up from her chair.

"I think he should be suspended and arrested," she said. "I never heard such a pack of lies!"

"I don't lie," I said and I looked directly at her, letting her know that I was a millisecond from spilling the beans from Friday, and you could see the air go out of her as she settled back into her chair.

"Well, somebody certainly smashed those mailboxes. Thirty-two of them, to be exact," Mr. Allen said.

Mr. Kearns cleared his throat. He was always clearing his throat. It was like he had a permanent burr stuck in there and he couldn't get it out. "They were smashed with a baseball bat," he said, making it sound as if he were about to reveal the secret behind the Kennedy assassination. "You do play baseball, do you not, Nick?"

It sounded weird. Not Nick. What was a notnick? Somebody who was crazy about knots? I nodded apprehensively.

"It seems a little too coincidental," Mr. Kearns said. "Especially when we know your mother's car was on the scene."

"I took a shortcut back from the pizza place."

"Ah," Mr. Kearns said, "so you admit you were there."

"I never said I wasn't. It's a town road, after all, and a fairly busy town road."

He leaned toward me. "Who was with you in that car?"

The only name that popped into my head was Mark McGwire, but I didn't say it. Not that I didn't want to. I mean, I wanted to say that more than anything, but I bit my tongue and told them the truth. "Paul Hunter and Ronnie Lathrop."

"Correct me if I'm wrong," Kearns said, "but that road is hardly a shortcut from Caruso's."

I really don't like Kearns. When he talks it sounds like somebody's pouring oil from a jar, the words sliding out of him though a self-satisfied smirk. " We didn't go to Caruso's. We went to the new place on the other side of town."

"Any ... witnesses?" The words seemed to ooze from his pores. And you could see he thought he should have been a prosecuting attorney.

"Go ask."

"You know, Nicholas," Kearns said, "it strikes me that you need an attitude adjustment. You are very belligerent."

I sighed. "Look, I have to get to practice, so let's wrap this up. I know who smashed the mailboxes because I happened to see them. But I'm not gonna tell you who did it because if I do I'll get the crap beat out of me, and I kind of had an idea that I'd like to finish the year in one piece."

Kearns chuckled. "Remember we have a witness."

"No, you don't. You have someone who heard a noise, looked out, and saw a white Volvo wagon, and then you ran down every white Volvo wagon in town and found the only one with a teenager in the house. Just think how it had to have happened. Somebody is sitting inside their house, they hear a noise, get up and cross to the window, and by then the car with the mailbox whacker is gone and they see a white Volvo wagon because I was the next car."

"I told you he was clever," the Toad said. "Boys like him should be put in jail where they belong."

"Or maybe teachers should feed them tranquilizers or Ritalin," I said, snapping the words at her.

She looked like she'd been shot between the eyes.

Kearns grinned. "Yes, you are clever. Very clever. But the fact remains that we are offering you the chance to confess and you are not taking advantage of that offer."

I heard the trooper stir, his leather gun belt creaking as he pushed back in his chair. "This isn't getting anywhere. He's telling the truth," he said. "Nick, I'm sure you understand that we'd like to get these guys, but I also understand what you said about getting beat up. Technically, you are withholding evidence, but then again, you have a perfect right to act to protect yourself." He grinned. "And you're absolutely right. No one saw anyone actually smash a mailbox. They only saw the car."

"I turned onto Center Road because I was afraid that would happen. When I came to the stop sign there was a man walking his dog. He might remember the car. I think the music may have been a little loud. I also think there may have been some mailboxes smashed on Rocky Road after Center Road."

The trooper nodded. "Do you know how serious this is?"

"My father told me it's a federal offense. It was one of his conditions for me getting my license. I had to talk to the family lawyer about the penalties for stuff like that."

Suddenly Mr. Allen spoke up. "I agree with Trooper Gazerelli, I don't think Nick had anything to do with this, and I certainly agree that he has a right to protect himself." He looked around at me. "Nick, I apologize for this. And I congratulate you for your forthrightness. This was a most odious exhibition."

You could have knocked me over with a dandelion puff. The principal, admitting he was wrong? It was like having an alien spaceship land on the common.

The result was that I left the office feeling totally on top of my game. I'd taken the risk and I'd won. Of course, I'd been right, but it's never been clear to me that being right carries much weight with some adults. Nor did I believe for a second that it was over. And I knew there would be problems with the Toad, but once you convince someone that you're telling the truth, it's a whole lot easier the next time.

The trouble with that is that if you once get caught, and, most everybody who lies a lot gets caught, nobody ever believes you again. That's why, if I had smashed the mailboxes I would have admitted it.

Sure that would have produced a lot of nasty stuff at home and with the cops and with the people whose mailboxes had gotten smashed, but at least it would have ended. Lies never end. So you see, there's nothing goody-goody in what I'm saying, it's a matter of protecting your freedom.

Hey, I'm full of stuff like this. It comes from thinking, and I never worry about what other people think about people who think. That was last year, when I was a freshman. I spent most of the year trying to get along with one group or another, and all I got was confused. And Beth, my sister, my older sister, remember her? Beth was no help because she was very big into all kinds of complicated relationships, like you couldn't hang with this friend, if you were with these other friends, and you couldn't talk to this guy because he was dating somebody who wasn't on the list of cool people. Stuff like that. All lies. But I won't lie to you. It took me most of the year to figure it out.

It began with a question. What would happen if I just went my own way? That was followed by another question. What was my own way? Not a clue. What I knew was that I had two friends, Paul and Ronnie (who were equally confused) and beyond that I had a lot of people I knew. I also had nothing to lose, because for most of the year I couldn't honestly say I'd gained anything.

I did the unthinkable. I stepped back and took a look at what was going on. Now that was an eye-opener. I saw other kids acting like idiots, trying to act like they were cool. I saw them wearing certain kinds of clothes in order to more easily be part of some special group. Even so, the thought of not being part of some cool group terrified me in a way that I still can't explain, and even now I have bad dreams about it. But by then I had no choice. Once you look at what goes on, once you see something for what it is, things are never the same. And suddenly I was tired of being controlled by others. I got enough of that from adults.

At first no one noticed. They were so busy worrying about themselves that they simply didn't miss me. I ate lunch every day with Ronnie and Paul and in the spring I played baseball for the freshman team and I played video games and I never talked to anyone on the phone unless Paul or Ronnie called. I never worried about what I wore to school or whether I was having a bad hair day. I didn't even worry about zits. I stopped caring about what people would think because I answered questions in class, and I talked to anyone I pleased.

The last one was what got me noticed. Rumors started. One said I must be gay. Another said I had turned into a brown-nosing dweeb. Another said I had called Kelly Sparks a jerk right to her face, and because, in everything social, Kelly was in command, people said I'd signed my own death warrant. Actually, the first part of that was true. I did tell her she was a jerk. Here's how it went.

I was standing by my locker, dressed in chinos and loafers and a collared shirt, when Kelly and her adoring flock of fems stopped. Kelly walked over to me.

"What's with the clothes, Mr. Prep?" she asked.

"Nothing," I said as I closed my locker and turned. When you're face to face with a girl as good looking as Kelly Sparks, it is hard to stay cool. I imagined I was talking to a goat.

"You gotta lose the look," she said. "It is just so retro."

"Who made you the queen of clothes?" I asked.

"You are such a dweeb," said the goat.

"Really?"

"Nobody would be seen with someone dressed that way."

"Kelly, if you weren't such a jerk, I'd have to take you seriously. But because you are, I'm ignoring whatever you have to say." (Remember when I was talking about lying? I'm not lying now. That is exactly what I told her.) Worse, as far as the anointed were concerned, I turned my back on her and walked away. From then on my reputation was in the crapper and Kelly Sparks made sure it stayed there. She called me every name you can think of ... never to my face of course, oh no, it was always through her grapevine. I had some pretty bad dreams about that. In one of those dreams all the other kids were throwing stones at me. Here's what it came down to in the end. *So What!* I mean, like what could they really do to me if I ignored them? Nothing.

For a while even Ronnie and Paul acted a little nervous around me. They got over it each day after school but for a week or so they wouldn't eat lunch at the same table with me. Even that turned out okay because I sat at different tables all the time. I just spotted an empty seat and sat down. Once I even sat at Kelly's table.

"Do you smell something?" she asked.

"Yeah," I said. "Pits. I smell nasty pits. You oughta shower more often, Kelly, or does water wash off all your makeup?" I told you, I've got a mouth and I can think of things to say pretty quick, but never so quickly as I can once I'm on the outside looking in because then I don't much care what they think or say. When your nerves aren't eating holes in your brain you can think a lot more clearly.

"You are really gross, Nick. You oughta be condemned."

"By who? You? Com'on Kelly, own up. Between plucking your eyebrows and doing your nails you haven't got time for serious business. Just another bouncing bimbo."

It was like a tennis match. I was at one end of the table and she was at the other and all the faces turned back and forth with each crack.

"What do I care what a dweeb thinks."

"That's the difference between us," I said. "I think and you worry about how you look. Just another empty glass."

"And who do you go out with? Nobody."

"I haven't decided yet."

"And I suppose you think you have a choice?"

"Why not? I do the asking, so I get to make the choice. All the girls can do is say yes or no." I shrugged. "So take care of your nails and your hair, make sure your makeup is just right and one of these days I might give you a call. But don't count on it. I don't like my women all made up like a plastic Barbie doll." And with that I got up and left, looking for another table, figuring I had just dug a pit I'd never climb out of. But so what? To lose something, you have to have it already, and in the matter of girls, I had nothing. Just then. But I would, because that's the way it works. After all, most of the stuff girls like Kelly do is aimed at getting boys to notice them and then go panting around like dogs. Not me.

No panting. You don't pant, you stay in control. I'm not saying that's easy, because with so many hot girls around ... well, you get the picture.

☞   ☞   ☞

I've had better days, I guess, and I was kind of hoping that based on the way I had played the past Friday, things would go better at baseball practice. Instead, they got worse.

"Nick," Coach called me aside. "I want you to work with Heyman, get him straightened out at short."

I was stunned. I felt like I'd been poleaxed. And I was pissed. "Why would I do that?" I asked.

"Because I asked you to."

Coaches do not take no for answer.

"Why not just play me instead?" I thought it was an obvious and fair question.

"This is your first year on the team, Nick."

"But I'm a better player than Heyman."

"One hit doesn't make you a better player."

"So put me in the games and see how I do."

"This is a team, Nick. And everybody has to contribute for the team to win. You know the saying, there's no "I" in the word team."

"With all due respect, Coach, a team is only as good as its players. Heyman is a lousy fielder. He's afraid of the ball. He won't stick his nose into it."

"You can make him better. How did you get so good?"

"I've got a bounceback and last summer and fall I spent four hours a day working out on it. I still use it."

Coaches have brains with no wrinkles, and I knew a losing battle when I saw it. If I said I wouldn't do it, he'd either throw me off the team, or I'd never get into another game. I'd probably already said too much. I usually did. "Okay," I said. "I'll show him, but he's a junior, Coach, and he won't listen to me unless you tell him to."

"I'll talk to him."

It was my only hope. No junior will listen to a sophomore and I figured that I could piss him off so badly that when he got to batting practice his head would be muddled and he'd screw up there too.

I trotted out to short and I could see Coach talking to him, and when he trotted out he sneered at me.

"So, you're the wimp that's gonna show me how to improve my fielding?"

"Yeah," I said. "And you're gonna need a lot of work, because I never saw a shittier fielder."

"Lot you know."

"However much it is, it's more than you know. And anyway, you don't have a choice. Coach is watching and you'll either do what I tell you, or he's gonna ream you out and then you'll be on the bench and I'll be starting." It's a good thing that most jocks come with a strong macho streak. "The first thing you're doing wrong is that you're afraid of the ball."

"Bullshit!"

"Hey, I'm just telling you what I see, okay? You won't get your head down and you use your glove like you were trying to protect yourself."

"I'm not afraid of anything."

The way you work on the brain of a guy that age is to

accuse him of being a coward, especially if he is. I shrugged. "Have it your way, Dude, but I'm telling you if you're afraid to stick your nose into the play, you're gonna miss the ball. So you take a couple of shots now and then. So what? That's the game. Next thing. Because you're afraid of the ball, you're not ready to field it. When the pitcher starts his windup, get low, flex your knees, but stay up on your toes. Keep your glove low. Watch the pitch. Where it goes is where the batter is most likely to hit the ball. Never take your eyes off the ball. Watch it right onto the bat. That gives you a full step."

I waved at Billy Macklin, the manager, and he sent a ground ball right at Heyman. He made the fatal mistake for a shortstop. He waited for the ball to come to him instead of going after it. The shortstop is the most aggressive infielder because most of the time he has the longest throw and the only way he can cut that down is to go after the ball.

Heyman just stood there, and when the ball took a bad hop he was back on his heels and he couldn't react and the ball went skidding into the outfield.

"Move your feet," I said.

"Shut up!" he shot back at me, hissing out the words so Coach wouldn't hear.

"What are you, a statue?"

"I told you to shut up!"

"Okay." I stepped back into position, got ready and when the ball came I went in for it, moving to the left, picked it off on the short hop and fired to first. Nothing to it. At least there's nothing to it when you'd fielded about a million ground balls. For me it's an absolute rush. I never get tired of it. "Did you see what I did? Go after the ball. Don't wait. You gotta be hungry. You gotta want the ball."

He stepped into position, but he ignored what I had said. He was standing nearly upright, flatfooted, his glove up near his waist.

Billy hit a slow roller past the mound, just fast enough so the third baseman couldn't get to it. Heyman was two steps late and though he managed to field the ball and throw to first, the runner would have been safe by ten feet.

"There," he said. "That's how you field a ground ball."

"Except that the runner would have beaten it out." I signalled to Billy to hit one in the same place and he did it pretty well. I was off on the crack of the bat, fielding the ball on one hop, and throwing while I was still running. The ball smacked into Paul Brodeur's mitt with a good solid crack.

We went through that for probably forty-five minutes, with me showing him how to do it and then he'd screw it up. By the time batting practice started I'd pretty well worked my way into his head. As he started in, I said, "Heyman. If you're afraid of the ball out here, it'll be even worse at the plate." Mind games. Mind games work. But they only work if the person is angry. He came up to bat and started swinging and missing. The best he could manage was to foul off a couple of pitches.

I, on the other hand, was mister cool. And when I came up I nailed every pitch, driving them cleanly into the outfield. And then I got hold of one and smoked it, and I mean smoked it, and then stood and watched it glide out over the left field fence. Have you ever hit a home run? I mean, even in practice, there is no feeling like it, nothing. One second you're into your swing and the next second the ball is carrying high and far and it seems to take a long, long time to finally clear the fence.

Everybody was hollering and shouting, cheering me on as I grabbed my glove and headed back out to shortstop, figuring that I had about sunk Heyman's chances of starting at shortstop. He looked like a beaten dog. I never felt better in my life.

After practice I mended some fences with Coach. I stopped at his office and looked through the open door.

"Coach?"

"Yeah, Nick.

"I think you're gonna have to talk to Heyman. He wouldn't do anything I told him."

"Yeah, I saw that." He smiled. "I also saw you poke one over the fence. I didn't think you had that kind of power."

"Me either. "

"I appreciate your working with Heyman."

"He's still afraid of the ball," I said.

"Yeah, I saw that too." He nodded. "I'll talk to him."

"Thanks," I said and then headed out to the parking lot where Mom was waiting. It had been a strange and crazy day, the kind of day that wore you out. But when you come out on top, it gives you energy.

ELEVEN

Revelations

I saw Mr. Bede again that night, kneeling by the small
graveyard, his head bowed, and I had to swallow hard to get
past the lump in my throat as I thought of how sad he looked.
I climbed into bed, lying there, with my hands behind my
head, staring up into the dark of the room at the faint glow
from the stars on my ceiling, thinking about him coming home
and finding Mary all bloody and dead.

Nothing in my life had produced sadness of that sort,
and to tell the truth, I didn't much like thinking about it. In
fact, I tried not to think about it. But I couldn't stop. I wondered how much he missed his sons. Stuff like that produces
questions you can't answer, though in fact he had answered
some of them on Saturday. He hadn't spent his life moping
around, depressed, and making other people feel sad, even
though his sadness never went away. All you could do was
learn to live with it and go on from there. What a price to

pay. It had happened nearly fifty years ago ... nearly three times my age. It was a long time. I thought of him kneeling in the cemetery by a cold gray stone and ... and suddenly I was out of bed and back at my telescope, staring at the figure on the hill as it shifted and moved and slowly climbed to its feet, clearly favoring one leg. And then I watched it slowly disappear over the hill. Something was out of place. Something didn't fit. But what? I went over and over it, trying to make the picture come clear but nothing happened.

Stuff like that can make your mind whirl until you're dizzy. You know what it is, but you can't give it words, and if you can't give it words it doesn't exist, and yet, of course, it does, so you keep on thinking and trying to force yourself to remember. The harder you try, the farther away it goes, until finally all you can think about is trying to think.

I flopped over in my bed and lay on my stomach. I never think well when I'm lying on my stomach. Either one of two things happens. Either I fall asleep right away, or my mind begins to drift off on its own, one image sliding into the next and the next as I get closer and closer to falling asleep ... and suddenly I rolled onto my back and lay staring into the dark, wide awake. I couldn't fit the man I had met, the man who talked to me so openly and honestly with the man kneeling in the dark. It just didn't seem like the kind of thing he would do. But there was more. Mrs. Mason! Something about Rachel Mason, something about the way she walked. I remembered her standing and walking with us to the door when we left. Her arthritis was terrible, but she had not walked at all like the figure on the hill. Hers was a shuffling, gliding sort of gate, and he swung his legs outward when he ... no!

He only swung one leg. And that's when the hair stood up on the back of my neck and the chills raced like slot cars up and down my spine, because I knew the man out there was not Augustus Bede!

And from that I leaped to the completely unwarranted conclusion that the man I had seen was the murderer. I jumped out of bed and began pacing. It didn't seem likely. No killer would take such a risk. But if it wasn't the murderer, then who was it? I sat on the edge of my bed, trying to think my way through the questions that flew at me like ice nuggets in a hail storm. Who else was buried there? Were Mr. Bede's mother and father there? Could this be a brother? Nobody had mentioned a brother. Or was it one of Mary's relatives. Did she have any? I shook my head.

I slipped into my bed and pulled up the covers. In the back of my mind I had this nagging feeling that none of those possibilities applied. Even more disturbing was the feeling that I knew who had murdered Mary Bede.

It took a long while to fall asleep.

☞   ☞   ☞

Our school is not like other schools. It's an independent school and it's located on a hilltop and it's a campus instead of one big prison building. Just down from the school one of the oldest houses in town was being fully restored, and now and then our history class went there to watch while our teacher, Mr. Place, explained all about a whole lot of perfectly interesting stuff that never turns up on the SATs.

By now, of course, you know I'm pretty weird, but this is

even stranger. I think everything we do in the first three years of high school should be entirely aimed at the SATs. The only reasons I go to high school are because the law says I have to and because I'm too young to go to college. But college is where I'm going, and I think my high school ought to do everything it can to get me into college.

It's pleasant to find out interesting stuff, but it wastes my time. I don't care about having to learn stuff that doesn't count. I think teachers spend time on things like that because they're bored and they're trying to find ways to entertain themselves. Mr. Place was big in the Historical Society That's why he was interested in the restoration, and not because it was of any use to our class.

So, as he led us around the project, explaining about sills and lintels and mortise and tenon joints in the beams, I was half-listening. The building had been stripped to its original beams, and the ones which the termites had riddled had been replaced. Even the floors had been ripped up and you could see right down into the basement.

"Now, if you'll look over to the corner of the cellar," Mr. Place said, "You'll notice an old well. It was unusual for a house to be built with an inside well back then, and the owners have decided to restore the well. It is some thirty feet deep, all made of stone and going down into such wells is very dangerous because of the lack of oxygen. In fact, in the old days people used to store food in niches on the inside of their wells because without oxygen the food didn't decay.

"To restore a well, you have to first pump it out and clean it thoroughly. Then you work your way upward, making sure all the stones are secure. It's a long and complicated task and in an old well there is always the danger of a cave in. One of the things you want to remember is that when you explore old foundation sites where houses once stood, somewhere near the house there is a well, most likely covered with nothing more than old rotten boards and layers of leaves. More than one person has been killed by falling into such a well. You always watch where you set your feet."

Well, that wasn't going to turn up on the SATs either, but it was certainly good information and I filed it carefully in the part of my brain where I keep stuff that can kill you. By the time you're sixteen, that file is pretty big, but according to my father it never stops growing.

Later, in English, we talked about a short story we had read but I didn't have anything to say about it. Here is why. The girls loved it and the boys hated it, and the teacher, Miss Giles, loved it. I hated English, even though my writing mostly got high marks. We'd gone all the way through to spring and we hadn't studied any vocabulary or grammar. Most of the kids, even including Paul and Ronnie who were both in Miss Giles' class with me, thought that was great. No memorization. But here I go again. That's the stuff on the SATs, especially the vocabulary. After all, you have to have a good vocabulary even to know what's being asked.

But as school days went, that Tuesday was a coast. No quizzes, no tests, no papers due. Plenty of time for day dreaming and looking at the girls in class. The only disconcerting (SAT word) thing was that I was being trailed. The Toad was watching. Every time I turned around, there she was, staring at me and scowling. Say what you want, but something like that can get on your nerves. The only time I could escape her was in the men's room and you can't stay in there very long before somebody fetches one of the male aides to make sure you're not smoking or fighting. Now, the girls get into more fights than the guys do. You want to know why? Did you ever read anything by Charles Darwin? Me neither. But I did hear about him on a television special once. At Christmas, Beth was home and she's taking a course in biology in college, and she was into stuff about overpopulation and what happens to animals where there's overpopulation and how there are constant fights over food and other necessities. I put things together; overpopulation and survival of the fittest and the fact that sixty percent of the kids in our school are girls, and I think what's happening is that there aren't enough guys to go around.

I asked around and in every fight between girls that anybody knew about, the fight was over a guy that one girl had stolen from another.

One thing for sure, though, the Toad would never be in a fight over a guy because there wasn't any guy in the world who would want her, which is why she hated all guys.

Everywhere I went, she went. Even when I climbed onto the bus to head off for the game against Thurston, I could see her watching from her office window. Keep it up, I thought to myself, and you'll walk right into my trap. I didn't think she would, of course, because I didn't think any adult could be that dumb. Besides, at the moment, I didn't have one.

☞   ☞   ☞

Dad wasn't there and I wasn't starting. So? Nothing new

in that. And I didn't blame him. He had a job and that job kept us all in food and housing and clothes, and if his boss said he couldn't leave, then he couldn't leave. But I did blame Coach. There was no reason to start Heyman again. He knew it and I knew it and he knew I knew it, and therefore he knew it pissed me off and I couldn't think why he'd want to do that, or why he wanted to risk losing another game.

As we came up to bat I sat at the end of the bench as far away from Coach as I could get. I decided it was all about rules. As long as you had rules about what you did, you didn't have to think. Of course some rules were good, I mean you couldn't play any sport without rules, and in fact you couldn't get anything done without rules, especially rules about behavior. But coaches have rules like, always go with your older players and never admit you made a mistake. Dumb rules.

Baseball is a strange sport. Everything is one-on-one except the double play or tagging a runner out on a rundown. The notion of team play doesn't mean much except at one level. You have to believe in every other player who is on the field with you. When there is a weakness and everyone knows it's there, stuff begins to fall apart. We had a major weakness. Heyman at short. What that did was take away the pitcher's confidence because he couldn't count on getting a guy out on a ground ball to short.

It affected the batters because they knew the defense was going to give up runs and they were trying too hard to get as many runs as they could. So we went down one-two-three in the first to a pitcher we should have hit all over the lot. The guy had nothing. All he could do was throw it over the plate at medium speed, and all I wanted to do was get into the game and fatten up my batting average. I grinned. It couldn't get any fatter. I was already hitting a thousand.

They scored two runs in the first. A ground ball to Heyman went through into left. The next guy hit a ground ball to Dufresne and he turned to get the lead runner at second and Heyman missed the throw and it rolled way out toward the left field line and one runner scored and one went to third.

So our pitcher, Bobby Battersea, a good pitcher by the way, began throwing the ball higher, keeping it around the letters to keep them from hitting any more ground balls. He struck out one guy and the next one hit a fly ball to left, which scored the runner from third. Then Bobby struck out the last batter.

So we came up and Jack Brodeur singled up the middle and up came Heyman. Now the guy can hit, but what does he do? He turns up the power and instead of trying to hit behind the runner he swings through three straight pitches.

This is what team means in baseball. When a guy who is supposed to get it done doesn't get it done, everybody else goes flat. It gets even worse when everybody knows there's a guy on the bench who can get it done.

Next inning, nothing either way. The score was still two-zip when they came up in the third. And then things changed. Bobby Battersea, a senior who is going off to the University of Virginia in the fall on a baseball scholarship, changed his location and he fed the batter a sinker on the inner half of the plate just above the knees. It's the kind of pitch that produces a ground ball ... to short and that's just what happened. Heyman, of course, booted it. Then Bobby went back to his high fastballs and set them down in order.

We came up and Heyman led off. Now, to be fair here, a guy who has made three errors on three chances and struck out once will have a problem with his head. Everything starts to move fast and all you can do is react and because you can't slow things down you make more mistakes. Heyman had made three in a row and never got close to the ball.

Of course I knew what Bobby was up to. He was trying to get Coach to put me in the game, and well, it worked.

"Rivers, take short!" Coach shouted and I came off that bench like somebody had put a jalapeno pepper in my jock. And in the warm-ups I made sure I cranked the ball to first so it smacked like a rifle shot each time it hit Paul's glove.

I took the throw from the catcher, a nasty one hopper which only causes trouble if you don't get your nose into it. Easy pickings, though, when you've fielded ten thousand of them from your bounceback. I picked it off and brought my glove past the front of the bag to simulate the tag, and you could feel the rest of the guys pick up.

Usually the ball comes in from third, but I called for it and walked it in to Bobby.

"Thanks," I said and dropped the ball into his glove. "Now you can go back to your sinker."

He grinned and I turned and trotted back to short. Bobby is a sinker ball pitcher. He sets you up high and then he goes to the sinker and you can't get your bat down in time, and that forces you to hit a ground ball.

The first one came right at me, an easy two hopper and I moved in, picked it off and fired to first. It wasn't even close.

The next batter got under the high fastball and popped a Texas Leaguer toward left center, but I was off with the swing and I think I forgot to tell you that I can run like the wind. I also knew how to make that catch. You look only once and then run, hoping you've judged it right so you can catch the ball going away over your shoulder. I ran to a spot and when I looked up the ball was there. Sweet! And it did just what a play like that is supposed to do. It fired us up. We came awake. And Bobby knew the hole had been plugged and he could pitch to spots.

I kept hoping I'd get another chance. But Bobby was on top of them. Before I had come into the game they had a weapon they hadn't counted on. Once I closed the door, they crumbled. I've read about stuff like that, and I've heard the announcers talk about how important it is to have a short-stop who can take away base hits, which means make up for a pitcher's mistakes, but until that day I'd never seen it work.

It worked another way too. Our bats came alive and we batted around, which meant I got a chance to bat that inning. But luck being what it is, they changed pitchers when I came up. They brought in a tall guy, a very tall guy and my mind had been set on getting a shot at the short, slow guy. This guy was not slow. The only way I could think of to adjust to the change was to stand there and concentrate as he warmed up. I wanted no memory of the slow guy.

You always hear about how the harder they throw, the farther you can hit the ball. True. But first you have to get the bat on it and a guy who throws hard doesn't give you much chance to do that. I read in a book about hitters one time that the best hitters, the ones whose plaques line the walls in the Hall of Fame took what the pitchers gave them. They didn't guess fast ball or curve, they guessed zone and if a pitch was in their zone they went after it. Swing hard on the first two strikes, then shorten up and defend the plate and look for anything to hit.

But just as I thought my luck had given out, I got lucky. The first pitch, the very first pitch came in dead down the middle of the plate just below the belt and my timing was on. I don't think I had ever hit a ball so hard and it took off in a long rising arc and carried well out over the left field fence.

I heard a great shout from the bleachers and I looked around and there were Dad and Tom Baines standing and cheering away. I trotted around the bases and I don't remember my feet touching the ground. The whole team was up to greet me when I crossed the plate.

Stuff like that can do a lot for your confidence. It can also do a lot for your overconfidence and later in the game when I came up again I went down swinging. I got it back in the last inning when I singled to right, and I gotta tell you, the best hit was the single. I did that with my head in the game. Before, I had been in the zone and you can never stay in the zone. It comes and goes. But when you hit with your head in the game you can do it day after day.

By the end of the week, every guy on the team was using one of Tom Baines' bats. But by then a whole lot of other very strange stuff had happened, and yet somehow I managed to stay focused on both baseball and my studies. The funny thing is, I never thought about that. Some things cannot easily be understood.

Some can. Like the feeling of hitting your first Varsity home run when your dad is there to watch. Yeah, that can be understood.

TWELVE

Connections

When you become known as a jock your status changes instantly. No matter what went on before, your position in society rises beyond any understanding. But not with everyone. It generally goes down with the groups which don't like jocks and it goes down with teachers because they assume that all jocks are dumb or, at the very least, more interested in athletics than in studies. Who wouldn't be? Talk about instant recognition!

Of course that only works in some sports. Golf is not one of them. Paul and Ronnie were tearing up the links on the gold team and nobody knew a thing about it. We had been good before, but suddenly Paul and Ronnie had come into their own, both of them shooting in the mid-seventies and, from nowhere, we had the number one ranked team in the state in our class, and based on pure numbers there wasn't any team in the state that could touch us, but still nobody in the school knew anything about it. Still, the way I see it, you gotta sweat or it isn't a sport. Some of the guys who play golf don't even take off their watches! Of course, I knew better because I had spent a lot of time making an absolute fool of myself on the golf course where the standard jock approach doesn't work, even though the sport requires considerable athletic skill. I only played because I liked the game. I liked hitting the ball and watching it sail far out over the green fairways. But every time I tried to muscle up on the ball it went into the woods or the water or the swamp and disappeared forever into the place where all miss-hit golf balls seem to go.

Even baseball does not fully qualify as a jock sport. In fact the only spring sport that qualifies, at least in high school, is lacrosse, where instead of hitting a ball with a stick, you hit each other with a stick. All other spring sports are quite civilized, like tennis or track, and involve almost no contact with other players.

Dating is, however, a contact sport and it is very big in the spring.

So there I was sitting at lunch by myself because Ronnie and Paul had gone off early to a golf match clear on the other side of the state, and who sits down at my table but Cindy Bonney. I hadn't talked to her since the great dance debacle and I was still angry about that, and though she must have known that, up until now she hadn't cared. But now the word was out. I was a jock. I'd hit a home run. I felt like a mine that had been closed and now was being reopened because more ore had been found. Should I use the word golddigger here? Naw, too strong, and anyway, not quite right in its traditional meaning. But looked at another way, perhaps not so far off ... just a different kind of gold.

"I heard you hit a home run," she said.

I nodded.

"That's pretty cool."

"Just lucky," I said. "I got the right pitch to hit, that's all." I kept to my sandwich ... ham and lettuce on rye, a favorite.

"But not too many guys hit home runs, do they?" She grinned.

I can't help it. When a pretty girls smiles at me, I smile back. And of course, she was more than just a pretty girl. We had known each other since kindergarten.

"No," I said, "not too many."

"My parents were talking about you before dinner last night," she said. "They were having a drink and Dad always stays in the kitchen while Mom's cooking, and I was up-stairs so I didn't hear the first part of it all, but they were still talking when I came down."

Now there was an unpleasant surprise. People, adult people were talking about me. Stuff like that can be hazard-ous to your health. "What was it about?"

"I'm not sure, exactly, but I think it had something to do with the old crazy guy who killed his wife."

"He didn't kill her and he's not crazy," I said.

"How do you know?"

"Because they dropped the charges for lack of evidence and I know him."

"But doesn't that mean they just couldn't prove it?"

She was right, of course, so I nodded. "Have you ever

met him?"

"Of course not!"

"He's a genius, and a real nice man."

"That's not what my parents say."

"Why do they think he killed her?"

"Actually, most of that talk comes from my mother's mom. She was a friend of Bede's wife."

"What's her name?"

"Why do you want to know?"

"I'm looking into it," I said.

"What?"

I lied. "For a research paper."

"Oh."

I took a bite from my sandwich and thought about getting a couple more sandwiches before lunch ended. I never seemed to get enough to eat.

"How'd you like the dance?" she asked.

I have a terrible habit. Most of the time I not only tell the truth, but I don't spend much time beating around the bush. "I'd have liked it better if I got to dance with you more than once. That was why I went."

Girls are not used to that sort of talk. I don't know why. The only way to get stuff settled is to get it on the table. But clearly, in trying to make things clear, I had only complicated them more, at least based on her reaction.

"I never said I wouldn't dance with other guys."

"I must have gotten the wrong impression." But I knew I hadn't, and slowly a new idea began to form. Well, not an idea so much as another question. Had she gone around using the same stuff on other guys? Was it to make sure that enough guys showed up to make sure she had a good selection to choose from? Okay, so it was two questions. But it's hard to ask one question without another one popping up. I switched back to Mr. Bede. Not only was it more interesting, but much safer. The truth was, I had always liked Cindy and well, you know how it goes, you gotta keep your options open. "Can you remember what kind of things your grandmother said about Mr. Bede?"

"When I was little and I used to go there after school, she used to tell me never to leave the yard or Mr. Bede would get me. I was absolutely terrified." She looked at me, her eyes very round. "I do remember something from Christmas. The whole family, both sides, were at the house and I remember Grandpa Bonney saying that the whole town had got it wrong. The only man to be afraid of was George Paschendale and maybe his hermit brother Arthur. And then he told a story about Arthur Paschendale, about how he once tied up some guy named Winky Peals, if can you believe that name, and kept him three days in the barn before letting him go. And he said he knew a guy who served in World War II with him and they called him 'take no prisoners Paschendale.' Grandpa said that every time Arthur's unit caught any prisoners, Arthur would line them up and shoot them one at a time." She shook her head. "Not exactly a Christmas story."

"I guess not."

"But then Grandma Keene got into it and she said that everybody knew about George and Arthur, but what made Bede so dangerous was that he'd killed his wife and gotten away with it!"

That, I noted, seemed to worry a lot of women and I wondered whether they were all paranoid or maybe ... maybe ...well, something else anyway, even if I couldn't quite put my finger on it. "Pretty wild," I said.

"Are you really looking into it?"

"Yeah, and I guess that's what got your parents talking about me. I've been asking questions."

"How do you get the nerve to do that?"

I shrugged. "I get curious about things and then all I care about is getting answers."

She grinned. "Like why I didn't dance with you more?"

"Yup."

"I'm sorry about that, Nick. I don't know what happened. I meant to."

She sounded absolutely sincere, but like the old folk saying says, "once burned, twice cautious." Me? Cautious? Never! I just had really wanted to dance with her. "Maybe next time." And then I had this brilliant idea. Start a rumor. "Did you hear about Mike Oliver smashing mailboxes?"

"God, no wonder nobody would say who it was."

"Well, maybe it wasn't, but that's what I heard. And Hamm was driving."

"Those guys are really scary, Nick."

Suddenly I began to think that maybe it wasn't such a good idea. "Just don't tell anyone who you heard it from."

"Maybe it isn't even true."

"No, it's true. I got it from a good source. She said they were smoking dope and drinking too."

"Wow!" She laughed. "God, if the cops had stopped them, all the dope fiends in this place would have been out of weed."

Call me dumb, but all I knew about dope at school was that some kids were using it. I made up my mind a long time ago about that stuff after listening to Dad talk about people he'd known who blew out their wiring using dope. He said they'd turned into zombies, especially the ones who used acid. It, like, rotted the brain. Don't ask me why, but that really scared me. "I didn't know he was the supplier," I said.

"Yup. Him and Hamm. God, Nick, where have you been hiding. Everybody knows that!"

"How come he doesn't get ratted out?"

"Duh ... is everybody afraid of him?"

I hate it when someone does that to you. They have only one thing in mind, making you look dumb. But I let it go. "Does he sell the stuff right here on campus?"

"Uh-huh."

"But how? This place is crawling with staff aides."

"Betty told me that you write a question mark and your locker number on a piece of paper and stuff it through the front window of his car in the parking lot. Then he leaves you a list with prices, you check off what you want and mail it to a post office box with the money. Then between classes you wait by your locker with the door open and he walks past and tosses it into the locker."

"Betty's using dope?" I asked.

"No. Her boyfriend."

"That's pretty sad," I said.

"I heard you were against it."

"Yeah, I am."

"How about alcohol?"

"Everybody drinks some," I said.

"But you don't."

"No."

"You don't smoke, drink, or use dope. That's amazing."

"Do you?"

"No, but I thought most of the guys did."

"Ronnie and Paul don't either," I said.

"Even more amazing." She looked at the clock. "Gotta go."

"See you later?"

"Call me," she said and offered one of those Cindy Bonney smiles that I haven't been able to resist since kindergarten.

"Okay, I'll call," I said, and immediately hated myself for being so weak.

I bought two more sandwiches on the way out and stuffed them into my backpack. History was next and the weather was good, so I figured we'd be off on another field trip to the restoration and I'd have time to eat them while we walked down to the house.

And that's what I did, munching away and thinking about Cindy and nothing else. Girls can have that affect on you. No matter what else is going on in your mind, thinking about a particular girl acts just like a computer virus, wiping out your memory. And when that happens on a nice spring day with the flowers starting to bloom and the birds singing ... well you gotta be real careful when you're crossing streets.

It also makes it hard to pay attention in class and I could hear Mr. Place yakking away and I finished eating my second sandwich and stood there looking at the frame of the old house and wondering what I'd say to Cindy on the phone, when I saw something moving down in the basement and I turned to get a better look.

Someone had put up a sturdy metal frame over the well and there was a hose and a bunch of ropes running down into the well and a cable hooked to the metal frame. What I had seen was the movement in the cable as it began to wind around a big drum on the frame.

It seemed to be moving at a very slow speed, but I watched and waited and pretty soon a man's head emerged from the well. It was shaggy and gray and very long and smudged with dirt. Slowly, he rose up into the light. He sat on what looked like a boat seat with an array of tools hung from the side, and he looked to be quite tall and very thin.

He grabbed a rope and swung his seat off to the side of the well and as he slid off the chair his pant legs came up and my jaw dropped. He had a wooden leg and when he walked he swung it outward just the way the man on the hill had done.

He stood by the side of the well, picked up a rope and using a free hub on the end of the hoist shaft as a windless, he wrapped the rope around and turned on the motor. I looked carefully, counting six ropes lying along the ground and then a pile of muck and dirt on the dirt floor of the cellar. And there were two hoses, not one.

Mr. Place spotted me and walked over and looked down. "Now, this is especially interesting," he said. "That's Arthur Paschendale, one of the last men around who knows how to restore an old well. He has a pump hooked up to suck out the water and another to pump oxygen down into the hole so he can breathe. What he's doing now is hauling up buckets of mud and silt that have settled at the bottom of the well. He'll also check to make sure the sides of the well are in good shape and that there is no danger of a cave in."

Arthur Paschendale! *The* Arthur Paschendale!

Mr. Place called out. "Hi, Arthur, how's it going?"

Arthur looked up. "Good's can be expected." His voice sounded old and it squeaked like a rusty hinge.

"Find anything interesting?" Mr. Place asked.

The narrow face flirted with a smile that never quite appeared. "No. Just the usual."

I had my eyes locked onto him, watching closely. He appeared to be younger than Mr. Bede by several years and he didn't move like an old man. Even missing a leg he was quick and efficient and from the way he handled the buckets of debris he brought up from the well, very strong.

One question. Was Arthur Paschendale the man I'd seen at Mr. Bede's? And if he was, what was he doing in the Bede family graveyard? Were they related? It could easily be, I thought. Sometimes it seemed as if the only people in town who weren't related were new. I shook my head. No, it was something else, but my mind didn't seem to want to go there. I could think it through just so far and then it was like being swallowed by a dark tunnel with no light at the end.

Mr. Place went on talking, describing a lot of what he'd already told us, undoubtedly adding in a lot of other stuff, but I never heard any of it. What I needed to know was just where he knelt in the graveyard. Which stone did he stop at? But how I was going to find that out, I had no idea. As far as I knew Mr. Bede never left. Yet common sense told me he had to leave now and then, if for no other reason than to get groceries. But because I was in school I was never around when he went out. When would he most likely go shopping? Wouldn't it be when there were the fewest people in the store? Surely, he wasn't the kind of man who would waste any time standing in a line, so that meant either early in the morning or late at night. But I knew he was at home at night. Old people didn't like to drive at night and I remembered him saying that old eyes need lots of light.

One by one, Arthur Paschendale lowered the empty buckets down into the well. Then he slipped into the chair, pushed a button and the chair rose up past the lip of the well. He let himself swing out over the opening and slowly lowered himself downward out of sight.

The rest of the day, even including baseball practice, slipped by quickly. It took every bit of effort I could muster to pay attention in class, but baseball was easier. All the bounceback training had trained my mind to follow a moving ball. Even so, I was not truly sharp and I even booted a ground ball, which I never did. Everything else went okay.

Mom picked me up after practice and tried her best to get a conversation going, but I couldn't handle much beyond a few words. I just had too much on my mind. I didn't pay any attention to the strange black Honda in the driveway until I was inside and looking around for who owned the car.

Dad came into the kitchen as I was pouring a glass of milk. "Hi," I said, "whose car is that in the driveway?"

Dad grinned. "Yours," he said.

I poured the milk all over the counter, which Lizzie thought was probably the funniest thing she had ever seen.

"Mine?"

"A guy at work was selling his old Honda and I bought it and he dropped it off this afternoon."

"You're kidding! Is this a joke?" I grabbed some paper towels and began mopping up the milk.

"It's got a lot of miles on it, but it runs like a top and all the maintenance has been done. Mostly, the price was right."

"My own car? I have a car?"

"It's registered in my name because of the insurance, but it's your car, Nick."

"How much do I owe you?"

He grinned. "Three grand."

"You've got it!" I dashed for the door and out into the driveway, walking around and around the shiny black Honda. It was an Accord, a four door sedan, and it looked like a new car to me.

"It's ten years old," Dad said, "and it's got a hundred and fifty-two thousand miles on it, but it couldn't be in better shape. The keys are in it, why don't you take it for a drive?"

He didn't have to ask twice. I was into the driver's seat in an eyeblink and I backed it around and headed off down the driveway to the road. I felt like a prisoner who had suddenly been released from jail! I felt like a dog that had broken the chain that had held it to its dog house all its life.

I stopped at the road. Which way would I go? Ronnie's was closest and I turned right and headed for his house, driving as if the car were made of eggshells.

THIRTEEN

Bagging Miss Wortmann

I didn't go anywhere except up to the end of the road and then I turned right and after about two miles, right again and finally finished back in the driveway, sitting behind the wheel, listening to the radio and thinking about what it would be like to take Cindy to a drive-in theater.

Finally, I shut off the radio, drew the key from the ignition and hauled my badly overheated brain in for supper.

"I don't know what to say," I said. "Except for, thanks." I couldn't stop smiling.

"Your mother and I decided you were right about how convenient it would be to have another car, but there's some baggage. You'll have to run errands and help take Lizzie where she needs to go. One ticket for a moving violation and the car goes. I'm serious about this, Nick. And if I hear even a rumor about drinking and driving, you're through."

I nodded. "I'd have to be pretty dumb," I said.

"Yes, you would," he said, "although sometimes it's more a matter of temptation. The hardest thing to ask of a young man, and I speak from experience here, is to take on responsibility. We're asking you to do that. And we're asking you to get a summer job and earn enough money to pay us back for the insurance. Can you handle that?"

Again I nodded. What could I have said? No? I don't think so. "It's a great car," I said, wondering who was going to pay for the gas.

Mom took care of that. "For now, while you're in school, we'll pay for the gas and upkeep. Even when you have a job, we'll chip in for gas to cover any family errands. Is that fair?"

"Sure. More than fair. I can't believe it happened so fast!"

"It wouldn't have," Dad said, "if the car hadn't suddenly been available. I just couldn't turn it down. Every bit of recommended maintenance has been done. Walter Simpson is an absolute tiger about having everything on his vehicles working perfectly."

"Thanks again," I said.

Dad grinned. "Tom Baines tells me he's sold forty bats this week, just to guys on your team."

"It isn't *just* the bat, you know," I said, feeling as if my talent had been overlooked.

"Maybe not, but until you got that bat, you didn't hit many home runs."

"I *never* hit a home run before."

"So maybe the bat had something to do with it."

"Okay, well, I guess maybe it did. I got to thinking it was just the size and weight that did it, but he wouldn't have gone to all the trouble to have Mr. Bede make him that special machine if there weren't something to hardening the wood. Did Mr. Baines tell you how that works?"

"He did. Very impressive." He sipped his drink, an old fashioned. He always had one old fashioned before dinner. Never more, and it was the only drink he had each day. "How did practice go?"

"Fine. I booted one ground ball, but I hit the ball hard."

"You need a bigger hat yet?" He grinned.

I grinned back. "You saw what happened in the game on Tuesday. After I homered, I struck out swinging."

"But then the last time up you singled."

"My head shrunk back to normal size," I said. "It was my best at bat."

"That's just what Tom said. I think he was pretty impressed."

"So was I. I didn't know I could do something like that."

Lizzie walked into the kitchen. "How come Beth never got a car. Talk about sexist!"

That took the old folks by surprise I can tell you. It also left them nonplused. They couldn't think of a thing to say, except to kind of sputter like lawn mowers that wouldn't start.

"She never asked for one," I said, trying to help out.

"Maybe somebody should have asked her." Lizzie was laying groundwork for when she turned sixteen. I understood. It's never too soon to start. You mention it once and then again and again, so when it comes time, it seems like it was their idea. Was that what I did? Of course. I'd been working that ground since I was nine.

"She certainly could have had a car, Lizzie," Dad said. "But the subject never came up." He grinned. "And for her first two years at college she isn't allowed to have a car on campus."

I smelled a rat. "This is my car, right?"

"It would be nice if you let Beth use it too," Mom said.

I felt like somebody was jerking my chain. "After all the crap I've taken from her, I don't think so. And anyway, I paid for it."

"But what if she has to get to a job?" Mom asked.

"She's gonna be life guarding at the town beach with Millie and Millie has a car. It'll be just like last summer. Me, I'm gonna talk to Mr. Baines."

Dad sipped his drink, the ice tinkling gently in the glass. "We'll see what happens," he said, the tone in his voice signaling the end of the conversation.

After supper I got to take it on the rounds, first to pick up Ronnie and then Paul and we put on a few miles before I dropped them off and headed home. I gotta tell you I never had such a hard time concentrating as I did that night.

☞   ☞   ☞

Tuesday was very smooth. Word had gotten out about my car and that drove the value of my stock up even higher. All day long girls kept smiling at me and the only downside was that the Toad was still following me around. Something was up, but I couldn't figure out what ... unless she'd been called on the carpet and had decided to get even.

I decided to treat it the way you would if you were trying to figure out how a magician worked his magic. The key is to watch the hand that doesn't do the trick. So, I figured that

meant Kearns was lurking in the background somewhere. It
didn't take long. Somebody had told Mike Oliver that I'd
ratted him out and he and Hamm were waiting for me by my
locker when I came back from lunch. Talk about an up and
down day ... man. At lunch I'd asked Cindy to go out on
Saturday night to the drive-in and she'd said yes! I had come
back to my locker, just floating and there's the two school
thugs waiting for me.

"You know what we do to rats?" Oliver asked. Not only
was he big, but he looked nasty. His hair was thick and greasy
and he had a bad case of acne and very narrow black eyes.

"We smash them like mailboxes," Hamm said, grinning
the way tough guys do in the movies.

Another time, another day, I might have reacted differently. I might have ogled the muscles hanging out of Oliver's
tee shirt and wet my pants. But I was at the top of my game.
I was starting at short and Cindy was going out with me on
Saturday. "I didn't rat you out. You can ask Mr. Allen. I told
them I knew who did it but I wouldn't tell them because I
didn't want to get the crap beat out of me."

"How come Miss Wortmann called us into her office and
accused us of smashing mailboxes?" Oliver said.

"I'm gonna make a guess here, Mike. She's been trying
all year to find a way to get you tossed out of school, right?"

He grinned. "She's too dumb."

"Okay, granted, she's dumb, but she's also sly. And she's
after me too. So she calls you into her office and tells you I
ratted you out. You go looking for me, pick a fight, I defend
myself, and we both get tossed."

He didn't like the way things were going. He'd come looking for a fight he knew he could win and he was letting himself get talked out of it. Hamm just stood there like the big dumb ox he was, saying nothing.

"You know what I think," Oliver said. "I think you're a smart guy and you're trying to figure out how to keep me from squashing you."

"Mike, the last thing I want is to get into a fight with you. I'd get hammered." I looked him right in the eye. "But don't think you'll get off clean."

He was only an inch taller, no matter how much wider, and I could see just the tiniest flicker of doubt in his eyes, and I knew that he had heard about me hitting homers. What he wouldn't know, because he wasn't a jock, was how strong you had to be to hit a home run. I guessed he'd assume you had to be pretty strong. And he knew I was faster.

"So now you think you're pretty tough, huh?"

"No. Not like you anyway. I'm just telling you that if we get into a fight we're both gonna get tossed out and Wortmann wins. Is that what you want?"

Mike wasn't real good at decisions.

"Look," I said, "Wortmann made a guess that if I was afraid of getting beat up, you were probably the guy I was afraid of, right? I mean you've got most of the guys in school scared already, so that would be the logical choice."

"How come you're not scared?"

I hadn't thought about it! But it was true. I wasn't scared. In fact, I had this overpowering sense that I could take him. Talk about being on an ego trip.

"You're right," I said. "I'm not scared." I shrugged. "I figure if I'm gonna get into a fight, then I'm gonna get into a fight. No sense in being scared. But if you're gonna get into a fight, you ought have a reason. You think I squealed, and I'm telling you I didn't. Nobody did. I don't give a damn how many mailboxes you smash. That's your problem."

There wasn't gonna be a fight. The muscles in his neck had relaxed and his shoulders had dropped. And the odd thing was, I kind of regretted it. Go figure.

"What's Wortmann got on you?"

I shrugged. "I'm a guy. You know what the deal is. She hates guys. Especially she hates guys who act like guys. Any guy who does anything physical, she hates him. Look who gets thrown out. Last February they caught Jake Haversmith with drugs on him, right?"

He nodded. "Except that he didn't have no drugs. He says Wortmann planted them in his backpack."

"I think we oughta find a way to trap Wortmann. Who was with you when you went to see her?"

"Just me. Hamm had to wait outside."

I nodded and turned to Hamm. "Did you hear anything?"

"Yeah. She talks real loud. I heard it all."

"Okay, let's file a complaint, an official complaint. We'll give a copy to Mr. Allen and one to the school board. I'll write it up and if you agree, then you both sign it."

"We could do that?" Oliver asked.

"Sure."

"What if it doesn't work? She'll really be after us then. If I get thrown out my old man will kill me."

It was an idea I had never considered, if only because it was hard to imagine Mike Oliver having parents, especially parents who scared him. His old man must be a real brute.

"It'll work," I said, and then I thought of what else she might try. "But here's what you gotta do. Wherever you go, make sure you got someone with you."

He didn't get it.

"What she might do is claim you came to her house and threatened her. She might even spray paint nasty stuff on her house and say you did it to harass her 'cause she's gay."

"She's gay?" Hamm asked.

"That's what I hear."

"Maybe that explains the way she looks," Hamm said.

I didn't go there. No point. Hamm's brain did not make normal connections. "So, are we clear on this? You willing to take a shot at it?"

He grinned. "She's been on my back nearly every day. Twice she's accused me of using drugs, and I don't have nothing to do with that junk. You can't build a body like this and be doing drugs, you know?"

"The way I hear it, you're the guy doing all the selling."

He grinned. "Hey, somebody wants something, who am I to say they shouldn't get it."

"You're gonna get caught," I said.

"Naw, I got too good of a system."

"Are you making deliveries now?"

"I don't make deliveries. I ain't stupid, you know."

I nodded. "Okay. Tomorrow, right after lunch you meet me here. I'll have the letter."

"Okay." He smiled. "I like this. I like this a lot." He stuck out his hand and we shook. "You're all right, Rivers. I thought you were just another asshole like all the other guys in this place, but I was wrong."

Not till they were gone and I was alone did it hit me. I'd just weaseled my way out of a major pounding and wound up with the guy on my side. Maybe Mom was right. Maybe I would wind up as a lawyer. But I was also gonna wind up as a snitch because Gazerelli was gonna get a good big drug bust handed to him. I really do hate drugs. Nothing good comes of using them, no matter what anybody says. Heck, not even Oliver used them. He just sold them to other kids so they could wreck themselves.

☞   ☞   ☞

I didn't hit any homers that afternoon in the game against Kelly Tech, because I was not, after all, the next Mark McGwire. But I did get three hits and we won going away 10-2. Maybe it was the Strike Force bats, but nearly everyone on the team got a hit and I drove in four runs.

Mr. Baines cheered us on as did the other six people who had come to watch, and it began to look as if we might have a pretty good team, after all. Even Heyman got into it. Coach made him the designated hitter and he began to stroke the ball big time.

It's hard to explain about baseball and why it takes hold of you the way it does. No matter how hard I work at it, the work always seems like play. I can't wait to get to practice, I can't wait for the games. All winter long I think about the weather turning warm and the grass turning green, and always in my head I hear the sound of the ball hitting the bat and it sends chills up my spine. I dream of someday playing big league ball, of trotting out onto a field surrounded by thousands of fans. Through the worst of times those dreams never fade and they give me a place to go where I know what I'm capable of doing, and that is no bad thing to have.

☞   ☞   ☞

I met Mike and Hamm after lunch at my locker and they signed the letters and I gave them each copies. Then I put the letter into the envelope and sealed it and delivered one to Mr. Allen's secretary. The last one, I addressed to the chairman of the school board at his home, and dropped into the mailbox in the office.

Two days later it was like walking behind a manure spreader. I had called it. Somebody had spray painted the words gay and lesbian on the side of Miss Wortmann's garage and she had called in the state police with a story about seeing Mike Oliver, Hamm, and me running away.

But when the cops questioned us, we could account for our time and when they checked, our witnesses backed us up. Iron clad stuff. And besides we hadn't done it.

I sat in the office at the state police barracks with Trooper Gazerelli. For awhile, he didn't say anything and then he ran his hands over his close-cropped hair and sighed. "Okay, Nick, you wanna tell me what's really going on here?"

I pulled a folded copy of the letter from my pocket and handed it to him.

He read it carefully several times and dropped it onto the desk. "You guys really play hardball don't you?"

"I give back what I get."

"Yeah, I see that." He grinned. "Who got this letter?"

"Mr. Allen and the chairman of the school board."

He nodded. "Anything happen since you sent it?"

"Nothing."

"Pretty smart to have been so careful, I mean, making sure you could account for your time."

"I told Mike and Hamm that something like this might happen. I read about something similar in the newspaper once."

"We've got nothing to hold you on, but I'd like you to talk to one of our detectives. Can you wait a few minutes?"

"Sure."

He stood up. "I'll tell the other guys they can go, and I'll tell all your parents that there is nothing to the charges. Fair enough?"

"Sure."

A few minutes later he came back with a tall, gray haired man, slender, and slow moving as a cat, and he had very hard blue eyes that gave you the feeling they had seen all there was to see.

I stood and we shook hands. His name was Lieutenant Tom Trekker. And after Trooper Gazerelli introduced us and left, he read the letter and asked me again about what I had told Trooper Gazerelli. After I'd finished, he sat with his legs crossed, thinking it over.

"Either you're telling the truth," he said, "or you're a whole lot more clever than the average criminal."

"It's the truth," I said. "I won't deny I want to get Miss Wortmann thrown out. I won't deny I thought of a whole bunch of ways to make it happen, but I didn't have to do anything here. She did it herself. And I'll bet anything that if you search her house you'll find a spray can."

"Just how far would you go to get even with her?"

"I wouldn't break the law."

"That still leaves quite a bit of room."

"I don't want any trouble. I don't smoke, do drugs, or even drink. I just want to play baseball and get grades good enough to get into college. The problem with Miss Wortmann is that she hates guys. Girls never get thrown out. They get into fights, they get caught with drugs, and they get a slap on the wrist, but they never get thrown out of school. Only guys."

"Not very fair."

"No."

"I'd appreciate it if you wouldn't mention this conversation to any one, and I mean anyone."

"Yes, sir." I shifted in my chair, trying to decide whether to tell him about Oliver. I decided to wait. I had enough to take care of and I wanted Oliver to cool off completely.

And that's the way it was left. There were some questions at home, but my parents were on my side and Dad was even considering hiring a lawyer once the police finished investigating.

What's amazing is that none of this affected me all that much. I continued to study and play ball and I was getting better at both.

FOURTEEN

Into The Breach

Thursday morning I woke up with the collywobbles which is what other people call an upset stomach. I must have looked pretty sick, even though I wasn't running a fever, because Mom let me stay home. But she wasn't happy. Every Thursday, at noon, she plays tennis. It's kind of like a religious event, to hear her talk about it, and I guess she figured she was going to have to cancel. But I made a miraculous recovery and by mid-morning I told her she didn't have to stay home on my account. By twelve forty-five the house was mine.

Video games! As soon as she left the driveway, I headed for the den, cranked up Zelda, and started. I love that game and I expected to slide right into my video game zone but I didn't. My mind was somewhere else and finally I quit and walked out to the kitchen and stood looking out the window at my bounceback and thinking about the batting cage again. I wondered if Dad remembered our talk about building a pitching machine and I decided he probably didn't, but to be honest, with Dad, you could never tell. He'd turned out to be a whole lot smarter than I thought he was when I was younger, though he still had a few things to work on.

A stone wall runs along the back edge of our property, separating it from a big hay field that gets cut twice a year by one of the dairy farmers in town. Maybe it was the stones in the wall, but suddenly I was thinking about Arthur Paschendale coming up out of that stone-lined well and wondering just what his relationship was to Mary Bede.

How could I get at that? How could ... another connection, this one with the song I had heard at the new pizza place. At first, because it seemed pretty random, I let it go but it came back as if my mind wanted me to work on it some more. Finally, it produced a question. Had Arthur Paschendale had a thing for Mary Bede? Why not? Every guy in town had. Then I remembered seeing a movie about obsessions and how this guy, who was a stalker, had a whole collection of pictures of the woman he was stalking.

Only one way to find out. Check Arthur's cabin. Now there was a dangerous thought. But dangerous or not, it sent me scuttling back upstairs to change out of my PJ's and into jeans, a tee shirt, a light jacket, and Nikes and then I shot back downstairs and out to my car. MY CAR! Magic words.

The orchard was only about three miles away and I made sure to go past the restoration. His truck was there and I assumed he was working on the well, and that gave me some time to check things out.

But what I had thought would be pretty easy, turned out, like everything that looks easy at first, to be anything but. I found the orchard and a road that led back up to a cabin set well above the road, but I couldn't find a place to park without someone from the farm seeing the car. Any car parked along a country road sticks out like a zit in the middle of your nose, so I drove past and for the next mile there was no place to turn off or even turn around.

I drove on a way, wondering where the road went. It's amazing how you can ride around with your parents for years and never think about how to get from place to place. And then you get behind the wheel and suddenly you don't have any idea where you are. By then I was a couple of miles away and going in the wrong direction. I decided to do the safest thing and turn around. But I had already begun forming another plan. Paul's house was about halfway between home and the orchard. We could go jogging in the evening, late enough so it would be dark by the time we reached the orchard, and then I could sneak up through the dark and look in the windows. Dogs. Were there dogs around? Didn't every farm have dogs? I couldn't remember having seen a dog when we stopped to buy apples but even a sleepy old dog might bark. Worse, running around in the dark was a bad idea. It was just too easy to twist an ankle or maybe tear up a knee, and jocks worry about stuff like that all the time.

I turned and started back and as I drove I noticed how sharply the land rose up to the orchard on that side of the road. I stopped and climbed out. From here the car could not be seen, and I climbed up the bank, using the trunks of some big old trees as a screen. The cabin sat maybe two hundred yards away and a stand of thick pines screened it from the house.

Okay, risk time. I walked back down to the road, followed it for a hundred yards or so, and turned up into the orchard. Neat rows of trees stretched up and over the hill, all of them sweeping to the sides, the tops neatly pruned away. Bare ground surrounded each tree and the grass, which grew everywhere else, was only ankle deep. It left me no place to hide. I stopped and listened and I could hear a tractor in the distance on the far side of the hill.

I walked up into the orchard until I was parallel with the cabin and then turned. Despite the cool air I was beginning to sweat and my heart beat so hard I could hear it hammering in my ears. All the knowledge I had told me he wasn't there, and that no one else was there, but never mind. Until I knew that, I'd sweat. Slowly, I drew closer and closer, keeping the trees between me and the lone window in the side of the cabin. My pace had slowed to a crawl and I had to make myself put one foot in front of the other. It was like learning to walk all over again.

The sudden flash of movement, the roaring sound, so startled me that I fell backward into the grass as a big cock pheasant burst upward, crowing like a rooster, and flew diagonally across the field. I shook my head and sat there in the grass, waiting for my heart to slow. I began to wonder whether this was such a good idea after all. I was okay out here in the orchard where I could maneuver and run, but once inside I'd be trapped. The more logic I applied to my decision, the more I saw how idiotic it was to break into someone's house. And for what? To prove who had murdered Mary Bede nearly fifty years ago? Completely nuts. Not even a total fool would risk his neck to prove something like that.

Call me a fool, then. I had to prove it. I don't know why.
Sometimes there are things you just have to do. I shook my
head. What crap. Anyone who gets themselves into that corner is probably not gonna stay in one piece for very long.
Everything can be put off. Everything can be delayed at least
long enough to measure the risks, to make sure that the end
you seek justifies the risk. Like asking Cindy to go to the
Rialto. The risk was that she'd say no and I would have felt
pretty bad for awhile. But I'd have recovered from that, so
the risk had been small. Here I was dealing with a maniac. I
was dealing with "take no prisoners" Arthur Paschendale.
Feeling bad in a situation like this could be a whole lot worse
than just feeling bad, it could be feeling nothing, ever again.

For the last hundred feet there was no cover at all and
anyone looking out the window could see me coming. I backed
off down a row of trees and then worked my way uphill until
I could aim at the corner of the house. To see me from here,
anyone inside would have to open the window and stick their
head out. And from here I could see a back door. Okay, nothing to do but to do it, I thought, and I started toward the
cabin, walking as casually as I could.

Nothing happened. The only sounds came from the birds
busy with spring and the distant huffing of the tractor which
seemed to have come no closer. I eased up to the door and
looked in through the window. It was very dark with only two
windows in the front and the one in the side, and with the
reflections in the window glass I could see very little. I put
my hand on the door handle and slowly began to turn. If
someone had reached out and touched me just then, I think
I'd have flown into pieces like a crash test dummy doll.

I had expected it to be locked, but the handle turned and I pushed the door open to the inside of the cabin. It smelled of unwashed clothes and unwashed dishes and pots and I stood inside and let my eyes adjust to the dim light. Slowly it came into focus. And I stood slack jawed with surprise. The walls were covered with pictures, mostly the same picture, and all of them were of Mary Bede. I probably should have left then, but curiosity which does a number on cats, also has an effect on people, and I began looking around. Besides, I had gotten this far without any trouble and I was feeling pretty confident.

In truth, there wasn't much to see beyond the pictures but I found an old desk and slid open the drawers and looked through the papers I found there. Nothing but invoices and bills and each drawer produced less that the first.

The lone bed, a long narrow homemade affair, lay along the wall toward the back and there was a single shelf on the wall above that held several books. I read the titles quickly, and stopped at a black bound book about two inches thick which had no title. I pulled it down and opened it to pages of small, neat handwriting. It was a journal, pages and pages, recording events in the life of Arthur Paschendale.

There was a lot of interesting stuff about the war and I had to force myself to keep turning the pages. I found what I was looking for some fifty pages in.

> Mary, Mary, oh dear and precious Mary, what have you done? Gone and married a madman and left me here to pine alone. At least if you had gone away perhaps I'd not have felt such pain as this but to have mar-

ried here and then stayed here is almost too much to bear.

How I have loved you, always, and yet you never once glanced my way. I watched you go off with others and I would have spoken up were I not so shy. God knows I tried, but the words could not be spoken.

I had hoped when I came home from the war in the Pacific you would at least feel pity for a hero so badly wounded. But you did not even come to the parade, the one day that was mine, the one day when the people of this town recognized Arthur Paschendale for the hero he was. I did not even care that others knew. I cared only that you knew and might at last smile or in some way recognize that I existed.

You did not, and I now guess that your position in society had something to do with that. I come from the most shiftless family in town and you come from one of the oldest and most respected. Your father is a doctor, mine is a drunkard. Your mother entertains the finest families, mine is a woman of shame.

And yet no man could love you more, certainly not Augustus Bede. Nothing but a big scarecrow of a man. All brains and nothing else. He never even went to war. He stayed at home like the rest of the cowards. What sort of a husband does a man like that make?

Oh, Mary, what have you done?

I skipped ahead, reading snippets here and there, most of them the same, the same pain and agony over and over and over. And then another passage stopped me.

Killing is nothing. It is something you get used to. In a war you get used to it very easily. The first time I executed several prisoners, only the first one bothered me. After that, they were just the faces of the enemy who had tortured and killed my friends. My goal was to eliminate them all. To make each one pay the ultimate price. Sometimes I couldn't wait for a battle and I went off into the night on my own and penetrated their lines. I found them in foxholes and tents and caves and I killed them all with a club so there would be no sound.

The number grew. A hundred, two hundred, a thousand before I lost count. Even when I came home I slaughtered my enemies. There was a man in West York, another in York. Some were not even truly enemies. They just had to die so that I could go on.

And someday so shall I kill Augustus Bede, the worst of any enemy a man can have. I will make him suffer the way I have suffered, though perhaps, as I think of it, there is a greater suffering I can offer him.

Again I flipped through some pages and stopped. It was different, angrier, and a good deal more terrifying.

I wish the war had never ended. I wish I hadn't stepped on that mine and got to at least finish what I'd started. But I get nothing I wish for. That is clear now. All around me I see successful people living regular lives while I am denied the chance to live that way. I am an outcast, a pariah, a leper, and they have made me into that.

But I take my revenge. Tonight Warren Burke will be no more. I heard what he said, what he called me. A crazy cripple. That's what he called me. Tonight when he comes out of Pete's Bar and Grille, I'll be waiting for him in the dark.

I'll use a knife this time the way I did on that Jap officer when I cut him slowly into little pieces, making him live a long, long time.

How many have I killed? I wish I hadn't lost count. But there would have been no point. A warrior never counts, he just settles scores. I have many scores left to settle, but I will have to take my time. Too many at once in one place and the police will get wise.

But in the matter of killing, I have no choice. It is my destiny to set right, finally, the wrongs that have been done to me.

Not until I heard footsteps on the porch did I react. I stuck the diary back up onto the shelf and bolted out the back door, leaving it open. He could not have seen my face or much else, and I was outside and running fast when I heard him shout. I ran up into the orchard as fast as I had ever run in my life. I ran all the way to the end, well out of sight of the cabin and then cut to the left and ran on a long diagonal down to the road.

I checked in both directions. I couldn't see my car around the bend in the road and I crossed quickly into the woods on the far side and, keeping out of sight, worked my way back toward the car. I had to assume he was watching the car. He would have checked to see how I had gotten there.

He was waiting by the car, sitting at the bottom of the bank and if I'd come up the road he'd have caught me for sure. But now I was below the road and only by chance had I seen his feet on the far side of the car. I was stuck. All I could do was wait and I was at a disadvantage because the man waiting for me had spent a whole lifetime waiting.

I sat with my back to a big sugar maple, and stared off into the woods. What a dummy. I had put the diary back on the shelf when I could just as easily have taken it with me. Of course that would have been stealing and I'd never stolen anything, ever, so I thought that was probably why I hadn't taken the diary. I thought it was kind of ironic that the one piece of evidence I needed, I hadn't taken because the rules my parents had taught me didn't allow me to steal.

As I sat there, feeling the sweat drying on my face, I knew I couldn't wait him out. That meant I had to think of something, and at first, as usual, I couldn't think of anything. Then, slowly, an idea began to grow. He hadn't seen my face. It wasn't even likely that he knew how old I was. At most he had seen the color of my clothes and I could change at least part of that because my jacket was reversible. It was dark blue on one side and red on the other. Quickly I stripped it off, reversed it and put it back on with the red side out. Down through the woods there was a stream and moving as quietly as I could, I worked my way downhill, turned and then started back up, making plenty of noise, the way anyone would who was just walking.

At the road I crossed to the car and walked around the back and then leaped away as I saw him sitting there. For an eighty-year-old man with a single leg he came off the ground like a rocket.

"Who are you!" he shouted at me. "What are you doing here?"

"I ... I was just down in the woods looking at the stream

to see if it was worth fishing." I backed up several steps.

He looked at me carefully, and I could see the fury in his eyes as he stared at my jacket.

"How long have you been here?"

"An hour, m-maybe less."

"Somebody broke into my cabin. Was it you?"

"Mister, I don't know anything about any cabin." I pointed downhill into the woods. "There's nothing down there but a brook. I'm sorry if I was trespassing but I didn't see any signs."

"Who said you could park your car here?"

"No one. It's a public road, isn't it?"

"Nobody is allowed to park here."

"I didn't know," I said. "I saw the stream last fall when I came to the orchard to get apples. Mrs. Paschendale said it was all right to fish it."

"Well it isn't! I own that land and nobody can go there."

"Look, I'm sorry, okay? I meant no harm."

He turned away suddenly and strode off down the road toward his cabin, swinging his false leg to the side. Then he stopped and turned. "Don't ever come back here!"

"I won't, sir," I said, and I raced to the car, opened the door, climbed in, got the key into the ignition, started the car, and drove off. I don't think I took another breath until I pulled into the driveway at home and parked the car in the turnout.

I knew one thing. I had to get that book. I had to know whether he admitted to killing Mary. What worried me most was that he had probably gotten the license plate number from my car and he would find out who it was registered to and where I lived. And then he would know that Mr. Bede was my next door neighbor. After that nobody would be safe. By his own admission he was a killer, and not just a man who killed during a war. Arthur Paschendale had no reason now not to kill everybody who might know anything.

I was wound as tight as a rubber band on one of those toy airplanes as I climbed out of the car and went inside. Still, there was a pretty good chance he hadn't taken down the license number. If he were going to report the car to the cops, he wouldn't have waited for me. He had been set to catch the thief by himself. But what would he do now? Would he have any reason to suspect that the pictures on the wall would mean anything to anyone? The question answered itself. In a small town asking questions gets noticed and almost certainly he would have heard the rumors about my going around talking to people.

Or would he? Who did he talk to? Could I risk that? Could I risk that he was such a hermit that he didn't talk to anyone? Damn! I walked back outside, climbed into the car and drove to Mr. Bede's, taking care to park around the back where the car could not be seen from the road just in case Paschendale began making connections.

FIFTEEN

To The Scene Of The Crime

We sat at the kitchen table, Mr. Bede listening closely as I told him what I had found. And then for a long time he sat quietly, his big hands folded together on the table. He looked up and nodded and pushed back his chair. "I'm going to get myself a cup of coffee. Would you like a Coke?"

"A Coke would be great, thanks."

He poured the coffee, added some milk, and got me a Coke. "What you've said has caused me some confusion."

I drank some Coke.

"In my heart I always knew it would turn out to be something like what you've described, but I could never see who. I may be an inventor, but I don't have a devious mind. I can never impute base motives to people. I seem never to understand how dangerous people can be. And even more astonishing, I have never tried. I suppose, with two boys to raise and a thousand interesting projects to work at, I just couldn't find the time. Or maybe I didn't want to find the time. Perhaps I didn't want to know. Most likely it is impossible to say why I followed the course I did, but until the boys were grown, I stayed focused on providing them with as normal life as I could. And by then, sixteen years later, when my youngest graduated from college, it was in the past. I had wrapped years of pain in whatever psychic bandages I could find. The anguish returned when Cory went off on his own and I was truly alone for the first time, and I would have done anything to have kept him near, but it is a thing a parent cannot do. Your children must grow up and go off on their own, just as you will, Nick."

There was nothing I could say. I was hearing words that one day would make perfect sense, but which now I could not form into something understandable.

"In the end, I worked. There was always something new, something interesting and, in truth, the boys came home. I went to their weddings and I visited when their children were born and I get along very well with both my daughters-in-law. I tried never to think about Mary except as I knew her. I kept her alive in my mind. And yet, always, I wished for revenge. Now, you walk into my kitchen and hand me the chance for revenge and I have no idea what to do with it."

He was way over my head. I knew what to do with revenge. Take it! No waiting, no messing around, just take it! And yet, yet something inside me did, in fact, understand what he was saying. "He should pay for what he did."

"I agree, but I think I can't be part of whatever happens from here on. Tomorrow I will go to the police and tell them what you've told me and they will handle it from there."

I nodded and finished my Coke. "I figured out something else," I said. "He comes to the graveyard behind the
barn on Thursday nights."

"That was the night he murdered Mary. A Thursday night.
Thursday nights have bothered me most over the years."

"I wanted to warn you. It's possible that he might con-
nect us. It's possible that he might come here to kill you."

He smiled. "No, I'll not worry much about that. Arthur
Paschendale is a man of limited intelligence. I think it most
unlikely that he will make any connection between us. No,
I'll go to the police tomorrow and let them take it from there,
though I do appreciate your concern. And, of course, I am
forever in your debt for the information you have provided. I
feel as if a great weight has been lifted from my shoulders."

There's a problem with my brain. It doesn't shut off.
Worse, as anyone can tell you, it's connected directly to my
mouth. "Why don't your sons come back here and run your
business?" I asked.

He looked up, his eyebrows raised in surprise. "I never
thought of it," he said. "I wonder what would happen. They're
both engineers, of course, and both very bright and they both
hold quite a few patents. I've got enough land for them to
build houses of their own, well apart from each other, and
every day I turn away work because there is just too much.
What a marvelous idea!" He laughed and it sounded sort of
old and dusty as if he hadn't laughed in a long, long while.
"And to think, you even hit home runs!"

"How'd you ... oh, Mr. Baines."

"Of course. He's so busy all of a sudden that he can't
make bats fast enough and he says it's all the result of put-

ting a bat in your hands."

"I don't know about that," I said.

"No need to be modest, Nick."

I shook my head. It was feeling pretty large again.

☞   ☞   ☞

What worried me, though, was that Paschendale would tear the pictures off the wall and destroy his journal. I had a plan. It was a good plan because it was simple. All I had to do was park my car alongside the fire house and wait for Paschendale to go past on his way to the graveyard. Of course, that depended upon him keeping to his habits, and after finding someone in his cabin, he might not.

Even if he kept to his routine, he would most likely lock the place up, and to cover that I brought along a pry bar and a big, heavy duty bolt cutter. A few lies had to be told because nobody's parents allowed them to go off on a mission of war. So I told them I was going to help Ronnie with geometry, and then I drove to the fire station at the four corners.

I hadn't anticipated that they would be holding a meeting, but that was so much the better because it allowed me to park among a bunch of other cars.

At least an hour went by and sometime during that time I began to think about booby traps. It was a real possibility. Paschendale had fought in the Pacific and the Japanese had been expert at setting booby traps, so there was a better than average chance that he had set some of his own. But where? I'd used the back door before, so probably he'd set one there, unless he guessed that I'd guess that, and then he'd set one on the front door or maybe even at both doors. Or, figuring that I would have to come up onto the steps at either door, he had rigged a deadfall, a snare that would pull a loop around my foot and leave me swinging in the air upside down. Or maybe he'd rigged a covered pit with sharpened stakes. There were a lot of possibilities and thinking about them made my hands sweat and my feet tingle.

I saw the lights of his truck and I slouched as low as I could in the seat and watched him pull up to the stop sign. In the lights from the fire house I saw his face clearly. As I watched him pull away, another thought popped into my head. Suppose his brother was standing guard. Very dangerous. Waiting in the dark, he would have an advantage.

I scratched my head and looked around, trying to think of a way to ... and that's when I spotted the pay phone on the fire house wall. I dug some change out of my pocket. Within minutes I had the number.

"Hello?"

"Good evening, is Mr. Paschendale in?"

It was his wife. "Who should I say is calling?"

"This is Harold Granger from the Boy Scouts and we're conducting a survey and I wondered if Mr. Paschendale could answer a few quick questions."

"Hang on, I'll get him."

In the background I heard her holler for him and a few seconds later he came on the line. I gotta tell you I was flying by the seat of my pants.

"Mr. Paschendale, this is Harold Granger from the Boy Scouts and we wondered if you could tell us what you think about the Scouts not allowing gay Scout leaders."

Look, it was dumb, I know it was dumb, but it was all I could think of. I mean, I hadn't had much time to plan. Well, I won't tell you what he said, because they don't even allow language like that in the movies.

The best part was that he hung up and I was into my car in a flash and down the road. Past the farm I turned off the headlights and turned up the road to the cabin. I decided against either door and went around the side to the window, figuring that with so few people around he wouldn't have locks on the windows. But a nasty guy like that was bound to have some unpleasant little surprise.

Beneath one of the apple tress I picked up a branch they had pruned off in the winter and hadn't picked up, and I used it like a long broom to sweep the area by the window, expecting I don't know what, but something! Instead I found nothing and I pushed up the window and slipped up and over the sill and into the cabin like a snake.

My eyes were pretty well adjusted to the dark, but it was darker still inside, and I waited until I could see. There was a wooden chair next to the wall and I latched onto that, planning to push it ahead of me. Then I took out my little flashlight and shone it around, trying to decide whether anything had changed. It looked the same, but how could I be sure? After all, the last time I'd been in the cabin I hadn't taken the time to memorize where everything was.

Nothing to do but start, and I pushed the chair ahead of me, hoping the legs would snag any hidden trip wires. A foot at a time I scraped the chair over the floor and now I was sweating hard. It had pooled in my eyebrows and it was running cold rivers down my sides and I think if anything had touched me I would have exploded like a stabbed balloon. That nothing happened only made it worse because the longer it took, the more it put me on edge, expecting at any second to tumble into a pit full of vipers.

Finally, the chair stopped against the bed and I shone the light up toward the shelf. The diary was there but to get to it I would have to stand on the bed and I knew how that would work. I grinned. It was a trap. No question. If I stepped on the bed it would suddenly spring in from the ends like the jaws of a shark.

All righty then, I said to myself, as I picked up the chair, raised it over my head, threw it down onto the bed, and leaped back. Not far enough. The chair bounced off the springy mattress, hit the wall, shot back into my chest and knocked me onto my butt. Feel stupid much? Yeah, big time. But hey, caution always pays. I set the chair behind me and stood up, thinking that maybe Arthur Paschendale wasn't very bright. I mean, it would have been a really great trap.

I climbed onto the bed, my feet sinking ankle deep and the springs creaking loudly as I reached for the diary and then stopped. Whoa. A perfect trap. The old balanced shelf trick. Take one item from the shelf and it upsets the balance and springs the trap. The possibilities were only limited by the movies I'd seen: a big blade that swung out and cut you in half, a shotgun hidden where you'd never see it. I stepped off the bed and looked around for something to knock the books from the shelf and spotted a broom. Perfect. I stepped to the end of the bed, grabbed the broom, and then, without getting back onto the bed, I swung the broom against the books and sent them toppling onto the bed. Again, nothing.

And every time nothing happened it made me sweat a little harder. Of course I knew that it could also mean that he hadn't set any traps, but that just didn't seem possible. After all, he knew someone had broken into his cabin and, from what I'd read in the diary, he was the kind of man who liked revenge.

I picked up the journal, shoved it into my jacket pocket and suddenly I knew I had to get out of there, that I couldn't stay even a millisecond longer, and I whirled and bolted for the window and in the dark I stumbled over something, crashed to the floor and rolled across the room into a set of shelves full of pots and pans and dishes and it all came thundering down with a crash that sounded at least as loud as if somebody had dropped a junk car from fifty feet up. I was dead. I was sure I was dead. I had to be dead, except that I didn't think that the stuff that had toppled onto me could hurt someone who was dead and I'd gotten hit in about a thousand places and every one of them hurt.

Okay. I wasn't dead. I had plenty of evidence. I hurt and I was still breathing and I was scared. I pulled myself up, feeling a little dizzy as I looked back to see what kind of booby trap I had run into. Man did I feel dumb. The chair. I'd completely forgotten about the chair! Paschendale hadn't set any traps, I had! And I'd made enough noise to wake the dead. I whirled around, climbed out the open window, and ran for the car.

Now I used the lights. It didn't matter. I had what I'd come for and I'd be long gone before anyone in the farmhouse could react. I spun the car around and raced for the road. I could see no car lights in either direction and I just wheeled out onto the tarred surface and accelerated. Not until I was a mile away did I let the speed drop back to normal. The last thing I needed was to get stopped by a cop.

By the time I turned onto my road I'd pretty much calmed down but I was still so jumpy that any movement along the road set my heart pounding. What really touched me off was spotting Paschendale's truck parked back up on an old tote road just down from Mr. Bede's. I turned off my lights and parked on the road instead of pulling into the driveway.

All the lights in the house were on and I walked up to where I could see inside without being seen. In the room opposite the living room, the room where the door to the hall had been closed the day I visited, I saw Mr. Bede, standing with his arms folded across his chest, staring at the floor. I walked around to the door and rang the bell.

He didn't answer and I tried the handle and the door opened. "Mr. Bede?"

No answer.

"Mr. Bede?" I stepped into the hall and down toward the room. The door was open and I stepped inside. Arthur Paschendale was lying on the floor, trussed like a Thanksgiving turkey. His eyes were closed.

"What happened?"

Mr. Bede looked around at me and shook his head. "It's finally over," he said.

"But what happened, I mean how did ..."

"It's a good thing you warned me, Nick."

He looked very pale. "Are you sure you're okay?"

"I think maybe I need to sit down." He stepped back and lowered himself into a soft, red velvet chair.

"Is he dead?"

"No. At least I don't think so."

"Did you call the police?"

"They should be here any second."

I pulled the diary from my pocket and handed it to him. "Maybe it would be best if you said he had this with him."

He looked at me as he closed his fingers around the small book. "It's all in here? Everything you told me?"

"Everything." I looked down at Paschendale. I couldn't see any blood, and even though he was breathing, he still hadn't moved, "What happened?"

"Odd. Very odd. I knew he would look into this room first because this is where Mary died. I sat here in this chair with my back to the door, but I could see what was behind me in that mirror." He pointed toward the far wall. "I saw him come in and I waited until he raised his club and then I ducked and hit him with one of Tom's baseball bats. I didn't mean to hit him quite so hard. I should not like to have killed him, no matter how much he deserved such a fate."

In the distance I heard a siren and I listened to it growing steadily closer and then suddenly a trooper pulled up into the yard and came into the house. I stepped into the hall and met him at the door. "In here," I said.

☞   ☞   ☞

Arthur Paschendale did not die. In fact he recovered, in time, and ended up being convicted of the murder of Mary Bede. It wasn't much of a trial. They had the diary in which he did, in fact, describe killing her, and they pulled some

DNA evidence from the club he had brought with him. The club also had been used to kill the two other men he'd mentioned in the diary and a year later he was convicted of both those murders. He never saw the outside world again.

It's odd about people and how they react to things. It's part of why I think all adults need regular mental health checkups. Instead of hating Mr. Bede because they thought he had killed his wife, the same people now hated him because he hadn't killed her. They hated him because they had believed he had. They blamed him for somehow tricking them into believing the wrong thing. It makes you wonder. How can the same people who are so big on making their kids own up to their mistakes, not own up to the mistakes they make? These are the kinds of things adults do that confuse their kids.

Not all of them were so unreasonable, of course, because it turns out that there are some sane adults around, which, if nothing else, gave me hope for my own future, which as every kids knows, means becoming an adult one day.

That summer I cleaned up Mr. Bede's yard and stored all his pieces of metal in bins in the barn where he could find them easily. He paid me, of course, and when I'd finished that job, I worked as his assistant, which meant that mostly I ran errands, fetching this and that so he could keep going. I think Dad was pretty jealous of my getting to work with one of the world's greatest inventors, and every night at supper I had to go over in great detail everything we had done that day.

Ronnie and Paul went to work for Mr. Baines making baseball bats and we played golf every chance we got, and by the end of summer I'd broken a hundred. By then they were both shooting close to par most every time we played. That gave them something to crow about and it evened things up after the amazing baseball season I'd had.

I also got to meet Mr. Bede's sons and their families when they came to visit during the summer and that fall I watched two new houses go up.

☞   ☞   ☞

There's one unfinished piece of business here. My date on that Saturday could not have been better. But I'll leave that to your imagination because I'm not one of those guys who kisses and tells. I mean, there are rules about such things, and a gentleman never discusses with others what happens between himself and the girl he dates. I wish I could say the same for girls, who keep everything and nothing secret. I don't know how they do that, but listen to the way girls talk and tell me if you really understand what was said. Here is what will happen. You will understand only what you were meant to understand.

All I know is that when school started again I ate lunch with Cindy almost every day and my opinion of girls underwent some pretty radical changes. Well, maybe not of all girls, but they certainly did about one girl.

Sometimes in my dreams I stand on the edge of a hole in the ground, looking deep into the earth, and I drop a rock to see how far down it goes, but I never hear it hit the bottom. I take great comfort in that, though I have no idea why.

About the Author

Robert Holland has a B.A. in history from the University of Connecticut and an M.A. in English from Trinity College. He studied writing under Rex Warner at UConn and under Stephen Minot at Trinity.

He has worked as a journalist, a professor, a stock broker, an editor, and from time to time anything that put food on the table. He hunts, he is a fly fisherman, a wood-carver, a cabinet maker, and he plays both classical and folk guitar.

While he was never a great athlete, he played with enthusiasm and to some extent overcame his lack of ability by teaching himself how to play and then practicing.

Sometime during college he decided he wanted to be a writer and has worked at it ever since, diverting the energy he once poured into sports to becoming not only a writer, but a writer who understands the importance of craft. Like all writers he reads constantly, not only because, as Ernest Hemingway once said, "you have to know who to beat," but because it is the only way to gather the information which every writer must have in his head, and because it is a way to learn how other writers have developed the narrative techniques which make stories readable, entertaining, and meaningful.

He lives in Woodstock, Connecticut, with his wife, Leslie, his daughter, Morgan, his son, Gardiner, and varying numbers of Labrador retrievers, cats, and chickens.